Kassandra and

Kassandra and the Wolf

by Margarita Karapanou

translated from the Greek by
N. C. Germanacos

This edition first published in 2024 by

CLOCKROOT BOOKS
An imprint of Interlink Publishing Group, Inc.
46 Crosby Street
Northampton, Massachusetts 01060
www.interlinkbooks.com

First published in the US by Harcourt Brace Jovanovich, 1974

Some of the material in this book appeared originally in *Antaeus, Bitches and Sad
Ladies* (ed. by Patricia Rotter, Harper's Magazine Press, 1975), *Fiction,
Shenandoah*, and *Tri-Quarterly*.

Library of Congress Cataloging-in-Publication Data
Karapanou, Margarita.
[Kassandra kai ho lykos. English]
Kassandra and the wolf / by Margarita Karapanou ; translated by
N. C. Germanacos.
p. cm.
ISBN 978-1-62371-697-4
I. Title.
PA5622.A696K313 2009
889'.334—dc22
200900-6452

LC record available at https://lccn.loc.gov/2009006452

Printed and bound in the United States of America

2. Miss Darry

Like every afternoon, Miss Darry, my Governess, had taken me to the Unknown Soldier* to play. I built castles and pies with my bucket in the sandpit. Miss Darry took her pink knitting from her pink bag and started knitting.

The night before, pretending to be asleep, I'd watched Miss Darry undressing. She had breasts like bells, and her hairs in front were light brown. She'd lain down on her bed, and suddenly I heard a kind of panting.

"Poor thing must be sick," I said to myself, and she went on groaning.

All of a sudden, from her breasts, she let out this cry, as though they were cutting her in pieces, and after a while she fell asleep sweetly.

That's what was in my mind as I made castles and pies with my bucket.

After a while, Miss Darry left, and Miss Scriven came to be my Governess. She had heart trouble.

---

* The Tomb of the Unknown Soldier is in Constitution Square, in the center of Athens. *Trans.*

3. Sunday

We live next to the Palace.

The King and Queen and survivors live in the Palace. At the big gate, to keep an eye on them, there are 2 Gentlemen-Governesses in white skirts* and red downy hats. All around, shining policemen keep an eye on the walls, in case the King and Queen and their children make a run for it. But *they* don't care at all: they have that huge garden to play in. Also they have those round Gentlemen, who look like turtles, visiting them every day, and so they've always got some company.

Our house is big.

Evenings, Grandmother strolls around the parlor, showing me the ancestors. They're sitting in armchairs because they're tired. Under each name there's a little light, and the frames are gold and full of holes, like cheese. And *there's* the General, his hand in his uniform jacket to undo his buttons, and his eyes aimed straight at the buffet.

"The General," Grandmother says, "restored order in Greece." I imagine the General tidying up Greece, putting Gentlemen and Ladies in drawers.

On Sundays, Grandmother's in the parlor, at home. Tonight, only Mr. Aris has come. He's pointy, like a pencil, an ambassador and poet.

*The Royal Guard wore kilts. *Trans.*

Dinner is over. Peter brings in dessert and coffee. Mr. Aris is about to recite. He recites. I like it and laugh, because every so often he ends with the same sound, and I've learned to play the game too.

"Cheese-please," I shout, but nobody laughs.

Mr. Aris looks at me, melting with elegance.

I run down to the kitchen to hide under Faní's skirts. Faní is washing up. She has no age because she's mad.

"You all stink," she says. "You stink. Your money stinks like your minds."

"Tell me about the War, Faní."

She sits on the stool; her hands plow the air, they become blazing torches.

"THEN," she roars, "when things were going our way,* and our songs had raised the stones and sky, that ass ambassador and two-bit-rhymer Mr. Aris dived under the table, shouting: 'A Historic Moment!' and your Grandfather said to your Grandmother: 'Sappho, my dear, it's time for me to die,' and he did his best to do just that. And we went into the streets, and sucked the air into our lungs like crazy—we couldn't breathe enough of it. As for the lot of you, you'd all become small, you'd shriveled to the size of horse beans."

Faní smells of blood. I nuzzle closer.

"You ruined us again. You ruined us, you bellyaching money-grubbers," she sobs, while at the same time bursting into song.

* Faní had clearly been on the Left (eventually the losing side) during the Civil War (1944–1949). *Trans.*

4

On Sundays, a man comes for Faní. "My guerrilla," she calls him. All of her strains toward him, ready to suck him in. He, Státhis, tells me about the War.

"I was up in the mountains with Aris,"* he whispers, his eyes going velvet.

"You were with our Mr. Aris?" I ask.

He shakes like a tree, his laughter rocking into Faní's mouth. She shakes too, the saucepans and plates laugh, the glasses and forks and teapot laugh, and the kitchen feels as though it's going to burst. Their eyes caress, and the kitchen creaks at their breathing. Státhis swells out like a peacock in the Royal Gardens. Faní clutches her breasts and squeezes them. They grapple and run off like blind things to her room, hands and legs like octopuses.

I go upstairs to the parlor.

"A drop of milk, my dear Aris? Now you must try these croissants. They're excellent."

I'm cold and hungry. I feel miserable, I don't know why. I climb up to my room to look at my new book. I cry as I turn the pages. It's about the North Pole.

* Státhis is referring to Aris Velouhíotis, commander of the armies of the Left. *Trans.*

4. Mother's Present

One day, my Mother, Kassandra, brought me a lovely doll as a present. She was big, and she had yellow strings instead of hair.

I put her to sleep in her box, but first I cut off her legs and arms so she'd fit.

Later, I cut her head off too, so she wouldn't be so heavy. Now I love her very much.

5. The Wolf

"Come on, let's look at the book with the pictures."

I'd run to his room with the book under my arm, and give it to him tenderly.

The first picture was of a wolf opening his mouth to swallow 7 juicy piglets.

It was the wolf I usually felt sorry for. How could he gulp down so many piglets at one go? I always told him that, asked him that. Then he'd put his hairy hand in my white panties and touch me. I didn't feel anything except a kind of warmth. His finger came and went, and I watched the wolf. He panted and sweated. I didn't mind it too much.

Now, when they caress me, I always think of the wolf, and feel sorry for him.

6. The Patisseries

I was out for a walk with the twins and their Governess. They were so alike it was as though I was going out only with the One.

We'd also taken our buckets to make patisseries. It hadn't rained for several days, and the earth was dry and stubborn.

"Piss!" the twins said.

I was scared.

"Piss, so we can make our patisseries. Piss, or we'll pinch your bottom. Come on, piss, fatty!"

So I pissed. The earth had never been so crumbly and the patisseries so foamy.

When I got home, Grandmother was in bed. She was wearing her lace *liseuse* and reading *Brothers Karamazov* from a golden book.

"How was the walk?" she asked vaguely.

"Piss, Grandmother, piss! Piss, I tell you!"

For three days, as punishment, I did not have dessert.

7. The Honey

One night in summer, when Mother had kissed me on the left cheek and said good night, she turned the light off, and I was alone in the dark room. Singing to myself, I put my hand in my panties for a bit of company. But I went numb and furry, a sweetness wrapped right around me, and I couldn't stop.

Faster and faster; I was going to burst. Candies like weights, like sugared almonds, rose from my soles to my belly, and I was filled with syrup. Thick honey trickled from everywhere, and I was drowning in sweetness.

All of a sudden, when the sweetness had blocked my throat, the house started to shake and rain began to fall from the sky. The earth opened up and swallowed the houses all around, one by one. I pulled my hand out of my panties quickly.

"Sweet little Jesus," I said, "forgive me. I'll never do it again. Don't cut my life off!"

But the earth all around was still caving in. Little Jesus was really angry this time.

So I put my hand back in my panties, and the sweetness came back. I sang to myself too.

While the house was disappearing in the holed earth, the honey washed all over me, and I died in sweetness.

8. Hercules' Party

Hercules was having a party. I'd been looking forward to it like anything. Miss Scriven dressed me in my tulle frock, which smelled a bit moldy.

At Hercules' party they had a big table all covered with foamy cakes and strawberries, red as cherries. I wanted to do pipi, but I couldn't hold it. It came out everywhere, so I went over by the strawberries and did it all over the shiny parquet floor.

I called Zakoúlis, who was walking by, and stopped him above the little pond.

"Zakoúlis, if you take one step from here, I'll slaughter you and skeleton you," I said.

When the party was over, Zakoúlis was still crying from the spanking he'd had. I felt a great joy, and I was bursting with cakes. My eyes were starry.

9. Merry Christmas

On Sundays, I believe in God, especially in winter.

On Sundays, I become a child, filled with joys and beautiful thoughts; I brush my hair 100 times; I become good.

On Sundays, when I wake up, I feel like turning into a dog, a cat, even a bird—to chirrup, fly high in the sky—or in the sea, become a fish, play hide-and-seek with friends in seaweed.

On Sundays, everything's ready to change: the table to become a chair, the clock water, and I to become Another: a bird with noiseless wings, or a mermaid with a gorgeous tail, teaching sailors to dive, then turning them to stone.

On Sundays, when she kisses me, Grandmother doesn't smell of sleep; Grandfather doesn't look like a coat hanger. The house softens, becomes good.

In the morning, the breakfast table is piled with goodies: toast and marmalade, sweet bread plaited into pigtails, candy and cakes left over from Grandmother's Saturday night at home, round cakes, long ones, cakes with sugar and cakes with salt, cakes with little *chantilly* men and other lovely shapes as well; and there are 2 slices of lemon pie too, at the side of the serving dish, and there are tea and steaming chocolate.

It's snowing because, since yesterday, it's been Christmas. Little Jesus was born too. He arrived on earth as a baby so as not to frighten us, and many dead broke out of the cemetery last night. It was his first miracle.

On Saturday nights, Miss Benbridge tells me the miracles in order. Last night it was the turn of the bread rolls and fish. Which is why I am now swallowing the bread and melting with sweetness. I make little girls and seat them around the table to keep me company. I put myself among them too, and we look at each other. I make compliments to them so that they'll love me. We all stare at the snow together, our hair is freshly brushed and drawn back, we're wearing pink ribbons, and we smell of soap.

I also make little boys. I pay one of them more attention than the others. I put freckles on him, and make his eyes completely yellow. I lean over to kiss him—

"Shut your mouth," Miss Benbridge snaps in English. "And stop staring at me with that stupid grin. Stop talking to your plate. Stop…"

I'm alone again. I stick my tongue out vaguely at Miss Benbridge because she's driven away my friends and lovely pictures. I act the ape at her, the Chinaman, and then the frog. In a picture, I cover her in dung, turn her into a horsefly and a cockroach, and, finally, I turn her into a water glass, which I throw out of the window.

I eat another toast. Goodness, all of my good thoughts, the lovely things I saw, my friends and survivors, all go down to my stomach with the toast.

"Amen!" I shout, crossing myself.

Time for Church.

Miss Benbridge takes me to hers, because God visits it more often than the others. Everyone speaks English there, and Miss Benbridge is able to communicate with God in it because he's English too.

We've arrived. We pause under the lace doorway. All the Ladies are wearing stockings with a seam; their bodies are good, without odors. They have left their odors at home so that they will approach God clean, their hands white and bare.

"Merry Christmas, Merry Christmas!" I sing out, tossing my cap in the air.

There's Zakoúlis in his green hood, Hercules, Nadia, and Becky. I run up to say hello.

The bell rings 3 times.

The Ladies enter, the children follow in line. Chairs shuffle about. Damp. The aisle fills with mud. We sit.

The performance begins.

Vicar enters on stage in a black frock and an organdy petticoat underneath, like a Marchioness. On his feet heavy shoes with laces, as though he's on his way up a mountain. On his head a little hat like an egg, and he's angry. He stares at us, we stare back. Time passes.

All of a sudden there's a thump—the Ladies have opened their books at the marker, and, like a cannon going off, they start howling. They sing so high that the colored windows crack. I stop my ears with my fingers and sing a waltz.

This Glooooooooooorious day,
This Gloriiiiiiiiiious day...

Their throats tremble as though sparrows are trapped in them. Vicar opens his mouth.

"Silence!" he commands with the one hand, and begins with the other: "Today, my dear friends—" he says in English.

We sit.

"—we shall speak about Noah's Ark..."

A Lady in a blue frock and blue hair hands out white sheets of paper and colored pencils.

"Try and draw a lollipop," she says sweetly but a little severely in English. None of us knows what the word means, so we all settle for drawing something from Jesus.

All of a sudden Vicar breaks into a run, bounds up some stairs on the right, and disappears.

"One day, my friends..." a voice echoes from high in the ceiling.

The words float around the church like balloons. I chase the voice with my eyes. I listen carefully.

"One day, my friends, God became *really* angry, because men were doing mad and capricious things. They leaped about and all around and didn't heed him, and when the sun came up in the morning, they stuck their tongues out at him. So he cast down rain and they were all drowned on the spot."

"Zakoúlis, pass over the green, will you?"

Zakoúlis pinches me, spits at me, sticks snot on my paper. I paint the grass purple, while listening to the voice. How I like Vicar hanging from the roof! How I like the colored pencils! How I like Sunday school on Sundays!

The Ladies bow their heads under the burden of love. Also so they can listen carefully. They have come so close to God that they seem to be hurting somewhere. They grimace. Some have gone down on their knees, clutching their heads in their hands to keep them from flying off. Something draws us all to the ceiling. If I go on loving so much, I'll swell out like a balloon and I'll go BANG and burst. Holding tightly to my chair, I think of a tree to calm down.

With my pencils I draw the Last Dinner: chairs all around, the Apostles right and left, and Jesus under the table so as not to be a burden. In the corner, Magdalene is painting her toenails and nipples green.

"Nobody's drawn a lollipop," the blue Lady says, looking upset.

I hand her my sheet. "It's the Last Dinner," I whisper. She looks at her watch.

"Meanwhile... After they had all drowned—and SERVE THEM RIGHT—"

The voice is angry. I cross myself and draw Paradise: little hills covered in grass, the Good sitting *en groupe* on the ground, talking things over. And there's God, in his white gown, making his morning rounds, handing out fruit and kisses. There, on that platform, he's reading the menu for lunch.

Whenever I'm flying to Paris to see Mother, I think I am in Paradise. That's what I'm thinking now as I draw my picture of it. There you are, high in the sky, with everyone looking after you. You are nowhere, and every few minutes they're bringing you all these trays with goodies, and patting your head. That's how it goes in Paradise. And when you lean forward to take a look outside, you see white and pink little clouds.

Then I draw the Virgin Mary. Her belly's right out there because she's having another baby. She's bored, so she has gone out in the garden for a break. She leans forward to peer through the fence, picks a fruit, and polishes it on her swollen belly.

Vicar reads through a list of the drowned, cursing each name in turn, while stomping his foot on the floor to keep time.

"Only Noah, who always heeded God, was left. He woke up one morning, and what did he see? Water, water everywhere, and, right there, at his feet, an elephant, 2 goats and a gaggle of fowl, all weeping and gnashing their teeth. So he set to and built himself a yacht, which he called Noah's Ark. Then he climbed on board with his animals and said to God: 'O my God, don't soak us again. We'll stay in Noah's Ark, and I, Noah, together with my animals, will make new men for you, new women and children too: we'll make poems and jams for you. We shall love thy neighbors as thyself; we shall always laugh and pet each other.'

"And that, dear friends, is all for today. To be continued next Sunday. Now, let us sing."

We stand.

This Glooooooooooooorious day,
This Gloriiiiiiiiiiiious day,
My Lord has come to meeeeeeee…

We sit.

"My dears, let us sing again."

We stand.

This Glooooooooooorious day,
My Lord has coooooooome
To saaaaaaaaaaaaaaaave me…

We sit.

"One day," the voice whispers. It's in a hurry now and bouncing off the walls. "One day, a shepherd lost his sheep. So he left his flock and ran off to find his lost sheep. He found it, returned to his flock, but his flock was pfffft-gone. So he left the lost sheep and ran off to find the flock. Back he came with the flock, but the lost sheep meanwhile had run off. All his life long he kept losing first his flock, then his lost sheep, because our good shepherd had heeded God's words: 'It is the lost sheep that is important. Leave your flock and run forth and search for it, otherwise thou shalt not enter the Kingdom of God, even though you be the size of a pinhead.'

A sob floats down from on high.

We sit.

We stand.

We sing.

We kneel.

We lie down.

We snore.

We sing.

We fall back in our chairs exhausted. The blue Lady comes around with a little tin tray, in which we drop ringing coins.

"For the poor?" a Lady asks.

"No, for the heating."

Vicar begins his descent. We are all singing in rhythm, while he dances *sur les pointes*, spinning around and around on the stairs, his frock opening out like an umbrella. We clap at every stair, we weep in adoration. Now Vicar has landed. He executes a pirouette, tosses his skirts high over his head, and disappears.

We fold our drawings and wander off to find our Governesses.

Outside, Miss Benbridge is hurrying on ahead. I notice her legs, her elastic stockings, her little white hands. It's the first time I've seen her from behind.

"But she's old and always alone," I think.

I want to kiss her darling little bootees, tell her my thoughts. Now that I've seen her from behind, so small and so close to God, I'm ready to love her. Again I glance at her elastic stockings. I'm burning, I am beside myself.

"Miss Benbridge—"

I clutch at her hand and shove my nose up her skirt. Squeezing her darling legs in my arms, I bite her thighs— they're like sponge. I worship her.

"You filthy child," she screams. "I can't stand you anymore—and we've just been to church too! I know you. Oh, my God, I know what you are. You filthy little brat!"

Shaking all over, she grabs my hair. She doesn't know what she's doing. Let me forgive her. Her darling little bootee kicks me in the mouth, knocking me over on my back in the snow. I secretly wipe the blood from my mouth. She doesn't know what she's doing—let me forgive her. I smooth down my hair and skirt, I smile.

As soon as we get home, she runs up to her room and locks herself in.

I take a stroll around the parlor. I try on Grandmother's fur and high heels.

I go to do pipi, and drop my drawing of Paradise into the toilet.

10. The General

I often went visiting with Grandmother. She'd have her white pearls and jewels on, and I'd be wearing my candy-pink frock and silver crucifix.

One day we went to see the General.

To welcome us, he'd quickly squeezed himself, pajamas and all, into his uniform jacket with the medals on.

He has his slippers on farther down.

"What's your name, my child?" the General asked.

"Kkkkkasssssandra," I replied.

"And you go to school? Which one, hey?"

"Tttto the Dwarf's Hhhhhouse."

"Are you good at lessons?"

"Nnnnnotsssogggggggood," I said, exhausted, looking down at his pink slippers.

"The child appears intelligent," the General told Grandmother confidentially.

"Yes, General. Except that she has this slight speech impediment. I really can't understand why—we all love her so."

I was going to say something about the medals, but the impediment stopped me. How would I ever be able to finish the sentence?

II. Hide-and-Seek

One afternoon Zakoúlis came to play with me and Konstantínos. It was cold and he was wearing a coat with a hood.

We said we'd play hide-and-seek.

I lifted Zakoúlis up and locked him in the big cupboard, near the ceiling. Then we forgot about him and went to eat lemon creams.

3 days later, they finally found Zakoúlis. He was still wearing his hood, but he'd gotten to be very small, like an olive.

12. Uncle Harílaos

Uncle Harílaos played chess in a very nice way. He played with Grandfather and I used to go and watch with Grandmother.

They moved these bits of wood here and there, then sat still and stared at the tips of their shoes for a long time. Then they moved the bits of wood again. I drank orangeade and stared at Uncle Harílaos' ear, which was right in front of me.

One day, Uncle Harílaos disappeared. They looked for him for a long time till they found him at Bátis, in the sand, under the sea. There was a rock around his neck, which he'd tied with a string so it wouldn't fall off.

I thought of Uncle Harílaos' ear then, which was hairy, and had a sort of yellow stuff inside it.

"He committed suicide," Grandmother told me, crying.

"He committed suicide," all the Gentlemen and Ladies in black cried, when they came home and sat around, eating those sugared almonds.

"It must be a new game," I said to myself, overjoyed.

13. The Bodies

When I went swimming with my Governess, I always stopped outside the place where they slaughtered the animals. They also had hangers all over, where they hung the bodies up by the head. On the ground, the blood was purple and thick and smelled.

One day, when it got dark, I left home and went down to the harbor, where they slaughtered the animals. I went inside and stopped. A Gentleman in a white smock, which was all red, was cleaning the knives and putting the bodies in order. He walked over to me.

"You like it here, hey?" he said, boiling. "You little devil."

He smelled bloody, and I replied, "Sir, may I see the bodies, and touch them?"

He took me close to a very big body and squeezed my hand into the deep meat. The Gentleman's eyes had red in them too, and the moon jumped out from behind him. He smelled of sea as well.

The bodies swayed slowly on their hangers, and the Gentleman grunted.

"You little devil, what are you doing to me? You damn little girl." Then: "Come here and smell since you like these smells," he said, as he unbuttoned his trousers.

After a while, they picked another place to slaughter the animals, because, they said, the bloodiness attracted sharks.

14. Aunt Pátra

I went with Grandmother to visit Aunt Pátra, who was in the hospital. From what I gathered, she drank a lot of something yellow, which stung as well. We had some of the stuff in bottles in the parlor.

"And when she drinks a lot of it, she talks rubbish," Grandmother whispered in my ear, as we were going up in the elevator.

"Now you be nice to her," Grandmother said. "Don't you say anything stupid."

"How come you got like that, Aunt Pátra?" I said, as soon as we went in. "You look like an old woman."

We sat in some high armchairs, and my feet couldn't reach the floor. My shoes kept coming off too, and I had to curl my toes to keep them on.

"How are you, Pátra?" Grandmother asked.

"Ah, my dear Sappho, I miss it. I miss the damn stuff. They don't give me a drop in here. I'm going off my head, Sappho. We said we'd show a stiff upper lip, my dear, but not drop dead in the process."

That's what Aunt Pátra said, and looked at herself in the mirror.

As we were getting ready to leave, I stood on tiptoe and whispered in Aunt Pátra's ear: "Don't worry, Auntie. I'll bring you some of the yellow juice tomorrow. But mind you don't tell anyone."

I turned and fixed my hair in the mirror, which was murky and watery.

15. My Friend Becky

My friend Becky came to see me with her Mother and I took her to my room to show her my dolls. We sat on the floor with our legs open.

"Let's see your panties," Becky said.

I showed her.

"Take your panties off," Becky said.

I took them off.

"I'll take mine off too," she said.

We went to the mirror without our panties on and with our frocks in the air.

"It's the same," Becky said.

I got angry.

I almost tore her frock off, and I threw her panties out of the window.

16. The Lesson

It's dark.

I look down into Irodotou Street from the dining-room windows. It's been raining since yesterday; people and street glitter. Peter's drawing the curtains, first the white ones, then the velvet. He starts in my bedroom at the top of the house, and works his way down. Now he's right behind me. (I don't know if he's seen me; I can hear him pulling the cord, and the velvet draws to in front of my eyes, cherry red.)

The house turns in on itself.

We sit down to dinner.

"Peter, my good man, every day I see you with sticking plaster all over your face. When will you ever learn to shave like a human being?" Grandmother says, pursing her lips and taking her napkin from its silver ring.

Peter serves. Roast beef and carrots sauté. For me it's spinach, to go poopoo.

"7:30 in the morning sharp," Miss Benbridge tells me every evening, her eyes filling.

In the morning she nearly goes crazy when my poops don't come on time.

"All my life I've suffered from constipation," she says, whenever she wants to say something tender to me.

Peter sticks his tongue out at me, wets his lips with saliva, opens his mouth, and shapes it into an O. I cough to choke down my laughter, then stare at the family's jaws (Grandmother's and Grandfather's) chomping up-and-down-up-and-down-back-and-forth-back-and-forth, pausing in the middle, and again from the beginning. I stare at the painting opposite me, the one with the nice nude. It's Renaissance—Grandmother has the moderns in the parlor.

I remember Mr. Strongilós: "Their colors match the pillows on the settee," he had said. "But that nude is lovely where it is, because, as you are eating, your eye desires to rest on something concrete—a nude, or a *nature morte*— in short: something familiar."

In the corridor we have a naked Lady who's as long as a noodle. Nobody can see her, there in the dark, so, nights, Peter and I creep up and caress her thighs.

"A Gentleman or a Lady?" he asks, but I'm not going to tell.

"I'm leaving now, dear," Miss Benbridge's nose calls from the door.

I'd forgotten. It's Tuesday, and Miss Benbridge is calling on Miss Hobson, Grandmother and Grandfather are off to play cards, and it's Peter who'll be putting me to bed.

"Peter, take charge of the child, and don't stay up too late."

Grandmother dips pearls and rings in the rose water, grabs Grandfather Niónios by the collar, and disappears.

We climb up laughing, me taking the stairs 2 at a time, pretending I'm a kangaroo, liking the creak of my patent-leather shoes on the parquet floor. I tell him that the dolls scattered on the floor remind me of Likavitós.* Peter kicks them under the bed, and caresses my hair.

---

* The wooded Hill, haunt of lovers, in the middle of Athens. See chapter 19, "The Collections." *Trans.*

"It fills with darkness when I caress it."

"And yours with fire," I reply as a compliment, taking his hand. He bends and breathes down my neck.

I grow nostalgic. I'd like to be in bed, sleeping, or I'd like to be getting my satchel ready for school. I sit on the bed and watch him cover the lampshade, the bedside table, and the window with black drapes. Then he puts on the black gloves (a Christmas present from Grandmother), and comes to me. I feel his knees gripping me, my nose at the height of his belt; I smell his cologne.

Looking down at me, he undoes the buttons on his shirt, one by one. The red hair on his chest rages, my hand's lost in it. Peter groans. The room is dark and smells of rain.

He lights a cigarette and gives me a puff.

"What did Miss Benbridge teach you today?"

"To peel a banana."

"Like a Gentleman?"

"No, like a Lady."

His knees go through me.

"Like a Gentleman?"

"No, like a Lady."

His eyes go tiger.

"Like a Gentleman?"

"No, like a Lady. Not like a Gentleman, like a Lady."

He'll never make me say it.

"'Like a Gentleman.' Say it, my darling, say it, my angel: 'Like a Gentleman.' It's easy. Come on, let's say it together: 'Miss Benbridge taught me to peel a banana like a Gentleman.' I can't stand it any longer. Say it, sweety.

Don't torture me!"

I draw him down, put my mouth to his ear.

"Like-a-La-dy," I whisper, making every syllable ring.

"You'll pay for that, my little cabbage. Go on, then. Run down and fetch the banana. I can't stand it any longer."

I bring back a fat one from the kitchen.

"You forgot the knife."

"I don't need a knife for the banana."

I'm pressing the kitchen knife tightly under my skirt, warming it like an egg. Then I sit down at the mirror and stare into it, a plate on my knees, the banana in the plate.

Peter kneels behind me. Our eyes tangle in the mirror; we let them wrestle for a long time, to forget ourselves.

And then we start.

First the chants:

Houli houli hikki douli
I hold the banana surely
A wolf sneaks in
He licks my chin
I hang his skin
On a crucifix.
Up and down
In and out
It's God I munch and
vomit for lunch.

I swallow down a mouthful. Peter slips his hand under my skirt, his hair tickles my neck. I stomp on the carpet to keep the beat.

I'll eat the banana
Gobbledy up
I'll grow tall
I'll grow long
Make it pointy
Make it fat.
I am God
And I say:
You obey
or I'll cut off your life
and your higgledy-piggledy wife.

I eat some more. It's a sweet mouthful, a sweet pulp in my mouth. It's so nice I caress my teeth with my tongue. I grow tall, I go sharp.

"My little cabbage, I kiss your feet devoutly. Your mouth is as high as the clouds. I see your little feet, white and clean on the carpet, and I weep, I melt, I am wax. I'll devour you."

He squeezes his whole body against me, on my back. I eat some more, swallow its furriness, its roots, and its skin, munching away and singing.

Houli houli hikki douli
A crow's in town
He gobbles the wolf down
God will drown
And lose his crown and piggledy.

Peter's trembling from his hair to the soles of his feet, his eyes closed, as he sings a prayer softly to himself, moving like a boat, and his mouth going all soft, and he forgets himself, and his face falls downward, nothing holding it up anymore, and I feel something hard in my back, like a knife thrust, and he suddenly opens up again and blossoms out, shouts like a baby without teeth, chokes, and all of a sudden withers on my back, slips down, and curls up on the carpet.

A white smell of angelness fills the room, trickles in my skirt. Drops fall to the floor, tangle in my fingers, tickle me.

"Say it," he whispers, licking the drops.

He covers me, warming me like a bird, all of him on top of me. I take out the Hopscotch Stone.

> Stone of God
> Stone of Christ
> Stone of the 12 Madmen
> Make me small again
> Make me walk again
> Among the many men.
> My shoes creak
> His eyes break.
> Come my Lord
> I bring the Sword
> And honey.

I swallow the rest of the banana, lick the plate clean, and Peter's eyes flutter. Then, with blades and spikes sprouting from the tips of my fingers, I rise to my feet.

He hides his head in his body and becomes a turtle.

I deliver the first thrust.

"With this knife, O Earthman, I, Queen of the Banana, will cut you in pieces."

I strike at his belly.

"I, Son of God and the Hopscotchman and the Holy Spirit, will cut off your fingers, your nose, and your moles."

At his back.

"Your nails and your nipples."

At his chest.

"And everything else that sticks out."

At his belly, low down.

"I'll drive out the Devil from you and turn you into a bird."

At his neck, I strike at his belly, his hands, his head, hair, chest. I strike rhythmically, swishes cut the air, whips and whispers.

"My little cabbage!" His voice breaks and wavers. "My little angel! You are God on Earth; your patent-leather shoes spew flames, your teeth grind in thunder, I kiss your little feet devoutly, I bathe them in ice and earth, I bathe them in gold and thyme and hay, and everything hard I can find. Oh, my God, I LOVE YOU!"

If I don't stop now, I'll cut him in shreds. He licks up the blood in the palms of his hands and on the carpet, washing himself like a dog.

"Say it, darling, say it. You'll kill me."

I kneel and put my arms around him.

"Like a Gentleman," I whisper, tossing the knife away. "But, like a Gentleman in a frock, with breasts and a belly like silk, and velvety hands."

Peter moans and buries the knife deep in his belly.

17. Good Work

Every Sunday, Grandmother went out to do her Good Work. She took me with her too, because I liked the ride. She also bought candies for the children in the school, and her handbag was swollen with the money she'd taken from the bank the day before.

The little children Grandmother was taking care of were poor, and they had no Mother. They didn't even have a Father.

Along the way, a load of workmen were building walls.

"Why don't you take a different route, Peter, my good man?" Grandmother complained. "I said we were coming out for some fresh air. I didn't come out to see workmen."

Ladies in ugly clothes were crossing the road ahead of us, lugging shopping bags stuffed with food.

"The sluggish animals," Grandmother said, turning the other way.

We also went down a street where little children were shoving their fingers up their noses and bringing out snot, staring at our car as we drove past.

"This is disgraceful. Why do they allow the streets to be so dirty? What riffraff, Peter, my good man! It's so depressing," she said, taking a white cigarette from her gold box. A silver smoke filled the car and wrapped around my throat.

When we got to the school, some fat, spick-and-span little children raced up to open the gate. Grandmother arranged her fur around her, and examined her nails, which were painted red.

"Ah, the poor things," she told me confidentially. "The Good Lord has left them unspoiled," and her eyes brimmed over.

I got out of the car too, upset at seeing so many fat, spick-and-span little children without a Mother. Not even a Father.

18. 3 Blind Mice

One day, I was very sick. I started making noises and swinging from the chandelier in the dining room. I bounced up and down, singing "3 Blind Mice" with 2 forks in my hair.

Mother was away, so Grandmother and Miss Benbridge consulted Peter, and Peter told them to call Father over immediately, and Father came to pick me up. He had a furry hat on his head and a black umbrella in his hand.

"My child, I'm taking you somewhere to rest," he said, trembling a bit.

Peter smiled, took the forks out of my hair, put my hat with the little cherries on my head, and kissed me.

"Bye, Miss Benbridge. *Au revoir*, House," I sang out.

With Father getting more and more trembly, we took a taxi. He was in such a state he forgot the address.

"We'd like to go to the Holiday-House-for-the-Good-People-that-Hang-from-the-Ceiling," I told the driver, and he took us there directly. The sly old thing—he knew the address without me telling him, and as soon as we got out, he disappeared—we didn't even have time to pay him.

I was standing in front of this House with Father, when 3 Gentlemen with toothbrush hair grabbed us, and before we knew what, we were in a white room, standing in front of a table. A fat Gentleman with a pencil was sitting at the table, and he immediately started asking Father all these questions.

Father burst into tears, saying over and over again, "The child, the child, the child," and chewing his hat, so Mr. Fat called in 3 snow-white Ladies with red crosses on their chests to sit around him so he wouldn't be so scared.

Then he asked Father why he'd got married, why he'd left his wife (Mother), if he dived into bed with other Ladies, why he was crying and eating his hat, and if he preferred a room with a bath or one with a shower.

I was beginning to feel upset about things, since it was *me* Father had brought to the House to rest and sing as much as I wanted, so I started crying. I knew it was my fault that Father was sobbing and leaping on the table and chasing the 3 crossed Ladies around the room and grabbing their chests and bottoms and tearing off his shirt, and so I joined in the shouting.

"It's me, me, me, me!" I hollered.

But nobody paid any attention to me. They grabbed him and put him in this ancient robe and tied him tightly behind. Father had turned into a kind of caterpillar. He disappeared with the 3 Ladies, who were holding him in their arms, and all the time I was sitting there, with my finger pointing to my chest, yelling:

"It's me, me, me, me!" and singing "3 Blind Mice" to them, and even doing my somersaults, and pulling my faces, but Mr. Fat just looked at me sweetly and said:

"Your Father will be staying with us for some time, my little girl," and he straightened my hat on my head and gave me some money to get a taxi.

I found one, got in, and sat back looking very serious. Then I wound down the window and took some gum from my bag to pretend I was smoking.

"Where are you going, little girl?"

The driver was laughing and I thought he was laughing at me. I was not going to stand for that sort of thing. I'd show him. So I kept him waiting a bit, sighed indifferently, just like Grandmother, looked absentmindedly out of the window, and said:

"Home, please."

19. The Collections

I often went for a walk on Likavitós with my friend
Hercules and Miss Benbridge. We always took a big can
with us for our collections. The tin smelled of candy.

We used to collect these long white transparent things
that had a sort of snot inside, and our collections got
bigger and bigger. They smelled sour, and when I smelled
them I thought of goats.

After a while, the can filled and overflowed and
wouldn't close anymore.

One day, we showed it to Miss Benbridge.

"Oh, noooo!" she screamed in English, and fainted.

Miss Benbridge was in bed for 3 days, and a Lady in
white came to give her compresses and stick some needles
in her arm.

They told us it was our can that had made her sick. So
we began collecting peas.

20. The Letter

Grandmother is lovely and still. Her sheets of blue paper are in front of her—the ones that smell like flowers in sugar. Tomorrow I'll take one and eat it. She also smells lovely, and her room is like a birthday cake. How I like sending the letter. It's like eating a piece of candy.

Grandmother waits, caressing her gold pen. My mouth fills with saliva and I begin:

> My Dear Mother,
>   You asked me a question in your Other letter. You asked me why I draw on yellow paper. Well, you're right. I'll do as you say. Now I draw on white paper with yellow lines. When I learn all the words, I won't need paper at all. I'll just send the words to you plain, or else I'll find a new kind of paper that'll be sweeter. Yesterday I went out with Peter. We had a wonderful time, then we came home again. My Dear Mother, when are you coming back? I want to kill you.
>   I am sending you a bunch of Ghosts
>   2 magic piggledies
>   and 1 flower
>   *Kassandra.*

"Have you got it all down, Grandmother?"

21. Grandmother's Advice

"My child," Grandmother says, "I'm going to give you some advice. In a few years you'll be a Miss from a Good Family with a name so high—and that is no joke. Then, from a Miss, you'll grow into a Lady, and when you're a Lady, you'll get to meet a Gentleman who'll want to make you his Lady. A Lady of your position should not have too much brains—it upsets Gentlemen. So, when a Gentleman speaks to you, keep your eyes lowered; listen—keep your eyes lowered, listen to him and don't answer back.

"Then, when the Gentleman takes you to be his Lady, when he puts on his pajamas and you put on your nightgown, and he stands upright and naked and then on top of you, don't ever show that you like it. Just imagine that you're in the parlor, cross-stitching swans and peacocks. If you like it so much you can't stop yourself, pretend you've got stomach cramps. Because if you were to moan, the Gentleman would divorce you and, with the name you have and the position you hold, that would be terrible.

"Always look as though you're in the parlor—drink tea and discuss what's going to happen to the children of the poor, and you'll always be a proper Lady."

I trot down to Faní.

"My child," Faní. says, "learn to caress. At night, learn the secrets under the sheet, open your legs and let the little stars and hurricanes into your belly. Learn the oceans and stars, honey and agony. Learn your body: learn to squeeze it, embroider it, water it, and kiss it. Learn to hug it. Learn to moan, cry, and laugh. Learn the secrets under the sheet."

Nights, now, I stay awake till morning. I never liked cross-stitching anyway, and I've got plenty of time before I become a nice Lady.

22. Before I Learn to Read I Pay a Visit to the Louvre

I've started to see words.

"Miss Benbridge, what are those scribbles outside the shops and in the streets and on the books going up the walls of Grandfather's study?"

"Words, words," she mutters, very bored.

On the way to the Royal Gardens, she stops to buy chocolates at a kiosk. A word like a snake stares at me: there's a pot like Grandmother's chamber pot, a mouth in the middle, and next to it a nail scissors. Then there are 2 little mountains like Faní's breasts. At the tail there's a ladder. I count the scribbles, examine them closely. I like this word.

But then, I don't know what it means. I get scared and break into a sweat. In the afternoon I've been invited to Zakoúlis'. How will I ever get there, if I can't read the street? How will I ever be able to live among words? When will I learn them?

Step, stool, table, garden, Zakoúlis, frock, Path, Grandmother-Grandfather, poopoo, and food—I collect all the words I know and put them aside in my mind so they'll be the first ones I'll write down when I learn to read.

That explains why I can't understand Mr. Strongilós' painting. I've spent hours staring at it, but I haven't been able to make heads or tails of a word like that: crazy scribbles, broad ones, wet ones—all paint and things—the one running into the other, and on top of everything, Mr. Strongilós, the sly old thing, goes and splatters green paint over them all just to confuse us.

Last year, I went to Paris to see Mother. She took me to the Museum. What a house! Not a stick of furniture, and paintings hanging on every wall. It was hard just to walk around the place, because every few steps some Gentleman or Lady, stark naked, was blocking the way.

I went out of my mind in there. All those stones and paintings stared at me, sometimes from in front, sometimes from the back. I got scared and started laughing, at which a Gentleman in uniform ran up and told me to shut up.

Lots of people were strolling about, talking softly—the way people do in the cemetery. I tried not to mind not knowing the scribbles and not being able to read the nudes and paintings, but, in spite of everything, I was jealous of those people standing in front of the stones and weeping for joy. In fact, one Lady grabbed the bottom of a naked Lady and looked as if she was quite ready to burst.

"I'll take you to see the most beautiful painting in the world," Mother said, grabbing me and pulling me away.

There we were, standing in front of the painting. Inside a velvet box I saw an ugly cow smiling at me, her arm across her frock, her hair hanging down like a mop, and she was quite yellow, like Faní when she'd come down with hepatitis.

The Gentleman explained: "From wherever you look at her, upside down, screwed around, doubled up, or whatever, her eyes swivel round and look at you."

I stuck my tongue out at her.

"You're insufferable," Mother said, pulling me by the hair with one hand and slapping me with the other.

"When you grow up, you'll like the Louvre," Mr. Strongilós is telling me a year later. "When you have completed your education, my child, you will be able to penetrate the mysterious regions of Art. *Ah, l'Art! Da Vinci, Greco, les Cubistes. N'est-ce pas, chère Sappho?*"

Grandmother smiles virginly.

"Mr. Strongilós, what about the people who'll never learn scribbles?"

He stares at me.

"Faní, the tea," Grandmother commands.

23. Jesus and the Virgin Mary

One day my cousin Konstantínos and I said we'd play. He'd play Jesus and I'd play the Virgin Mary.

I put the kitchen tablecloth on my head, and let my hair down. Then I wrapped the dining-room curtain around me so I'd have a long thing on. Konstantínos put the big saucepan on his head so he'd have a halo. He also took his shirt off and only kept his red shorts on.

I went down to the kitchen to fetch the hammer and nails to put him to death with.

"It's not his Mother that kills him," Konstantínos said. "It's a load of Gentlemen in robes."

"Same thing," I said.

I pinned him to the wall and stuck the first nail in. Konstantínos started screaming.

"Hey, what are you doing?" he howled. "We're only playing."

I raised the hammer again, after first tossing the tablecloth away. To get a better swing.

24. France

I'm in Paris to see Mother.

As soon as I set foot in her house, I came down with Asiatic flu, which, she says, is the rage in Europe this winter. So this afternoon my friend France is coming to keep me company.

France is the daughter of France's leading playwright of the upsurge. Tonight he's coming to have dinner with us, and he's bringing his wife Veronica along too.

France is old, nearly 10.

"*Comment ça va, France?*" I ask France.

"I'm in an awful mess, just awful, my dear," France replies. "You see, my little breasts are growing and Father's furious about it. When we went to the seaside last summer, he put bandages around them ever so tightly and fixed them with a safety pin. I looked like an ironing board. But that wasn't all. He put

> a woolen petticoat
> a pullover
> a pair of woolen trousers
> a pair of gloves
> a cap
> a pair of woolen stockings
> a pair of bootees
> and an umbrella

on me too.

"'Verrrronica,' he yelled at my Mother, 'tell your daughter that I don't want anyone ever to see her naked.'

That's what he said, Kassandra. Say, what do you want to be, when you grow up?"

"A policeman," I reply.

"I want to do a doctor's desertation on Strindberg."

"What's that?"

"How should I know? One day I heard Father screaming at Mother: 'Verrrronica, Strindberg is a cunt.'"

"France, what's a doctor's desertation?"

"Well, you see, you take a book and go to the middle of a desert or something and then you bury it in the sand for a long time and then you dig it up again and you find that all the words have got mixed up like the sand and then you put them all back in place only this time you put them back any way *you* like. And then they make you a doctor. And I want to become a doctor without having to cut frogs in two."

"Oh, that's wonderful, France. But I want to become a policeman and wear a uniform and a gun. You know something, though, you're going to spoil your frocks with all these desertations and diggings and things."

"Yesterday it was Father's premiere, you know."

"A dissertation?"

"No, silly, he wrote it himself. It's called *Rabies and Diarrhea*. We had a box all to ourselves, Mother and me. Well, up went the curtain and a Gentleman, a Lady, and a little girl started chatting away.

"'Hey, Mother,' I said, 'did you hear what the Gentleman just said to the Lady? Father said exactly the same thing to *you* yesterday.'"

"And sure enough, it was Mother and *me* hanging

from the roof of the stage, and we had wings on too, and Father was down below in a mousetrap.

"'Yes,' Mother said to me proudly, 'but *we're* in Paradise, while your Father's down in *Hell*.'"

France's Father and his wife, Veronica, arrive for dinner. They always arrive early because France's Father is so busy writing. Veronica is no taller than his shinbone. She's in a sailor suit, white bobby socks, and green patent-leather shoes.

We sit at table, me in my nightgown and Asiatic flu.

"A drop of whiskey, Eugène?" Mother asks.

"NO!" Veronica shouts.

"A little salad?"

"NO! The vinegar reminds him of whiskey."

"But I've dressed the salad with lemon."

"That reminds him of gin. My dear Kassandra," she says to Mother, "when he's writing, I cut a few pages out of the Bible and boil them for him with a sprig of celery."

"I'm going to become a policeman, Eugène," I announce. "France is going to do a doctor's desertation in the desert."

Eugène snatches the tablecloth off the table and everything crashes and spills all over the floor. Then he climbs on the table.

"Verrrrronica, I've already told you, Strindberg is a cunt. And tell your daughter that if she dares to do any desertations, I'll forbid her ever to say her prayers again."

Eugène climbs down from the table.

"Verrrronica, let's go, I'm hungry. I want a taste of the Apocalypse tonight—and this time not boiled. FRIED."

Next morning, I cut a few pages out of the Bible. In thick letters at the top it says Offering of Isaac. I drop them in a pan and cook them with chopped onions, just as I've seen Faní doing at home. I get diarrhea.

The Offering of Isaac pours into the toilet; I am beside myself with joy. I rush out of the bathroom, my bottom bare, and climb on the table, and, looking at Mother, I yell:

"Mother, Mother, I've just made a desertation!"

25. Aunt Magdalen

Hercules and I are inseparable.

In the afternoons, he comes over and we play Mothers and Fathers; we play doctors too. I'm Father and he's Mother. My doll Flora's the child. Flora falls seriously ill, and by the time the doctor, who lives in Siam, arrives, she's dead at least 37 times.

Today we're playing doctors. We've had our operations and decide to take a look at our behinds. We look behind. We're the same. We're about to look in front to make comparisons, when the door opens and in comes Aunt Magdalen.

"Auntie, why don't you come and play with us? We want to see what you look like in front."

But Auntie's shaking all over, she's gone quite yellow, and her eyes are popping out of her head. Suddenly she starts shouting, her eyes fixed on our behinds.

"What's the meaning of this, you filthy, obscene little brats? Get your clothes on this instant. Oh, God, forgive them," she sobs, clutching at her behind. "If you do it again, even if you do it in secret, God will tell me, and I won't be able to bear it. I'll die. I can see you wallowing in sin, both of you, stinking of the flesh. Fetch me behind me, Satan!" she screams, crossing herself. Then she fixes her hair a bit in the mirror.

We both burst into tears, without knowing why. Hercules' behind goes cherry red.

At 8 next morning, Aunt Magdalen's butler,

Vartholoméos, taps at her door with her breakfast, but doesn't hear her *Come In*. He knocks again and again, many times. Finally, he gets really worried and opens the door without Auntie's *Come In, Vartholoméos*.

Her head is clear off the bed, her legs are in the air, her tongue's hanging down to the floor. She must be laughing at someone: there's a grin splitting her face from ear to ear.

The funeral's at 10 next morning.

26. Family Dinner

We're having a dinner party, with guests. With plates, cutlery, 1 glass for water and 1 for wine. Faní's been cooking since this morning. At 5 sharp Peter draws the sliding doors of the dining room and puts on his white uniform suit and gloves.

Arrival: Uncle Harílaos and Aunt Pátra. Pátra fills her glass with yellow juice, and soon she's a hippopotamus. Harílaos starts playing chess on the marble flagstones in the hall.

Arrival: Mr. Stefanides and Bonnie. Profession: Member of Parliament. Hobby: Author. Since he was a baby he's been writing the *Revision of Greek History*, which, Grandmother says, is going to put a lot of politicians in their place—lying down, twisted around, and hung up. Bonnie and Mr. Stefanides are planning to get married. Though he's a Member of Parliament, he lives with his Mother, but he wants to have Bonnie so that they can brush their teeth together and go to sleep.

One day I was hiding behind the curtain.

"My dear Sappho, I don't want any scandals in the family sphere, you understand, especially now, when I might become the Prime Minister."

Which is why Mr. Stefanides and Bonnie are pretending they don't quite know each other tonight.

"*Ma chère Bonnie, comment ça va?*" he asks.

"A little mustard, Mr. Stefanides?" she replies.

One day I was curled under the table while Grandmother

was giving him advice about Greece and Bonnie.

"Grab 'em both," she said, fixing his tie.

Arrival: Mr. Aris. Profession: Ambassador. Hobby: Rhymer.

We take our seats. Peter becomes a ballerina with the serving dishes.

First course: Soufflé Français. Vin Blanc d'Alsace.

Aunt Pátra's on her 7th glass.

"A little soufflé, Pátra dear?"

Grandmother's voice rustles like her dress. She is so polite she turns into a painting in a golden frame, she turns into a *mature morte* of a vase, flowers, and some fruit on a table.

"Without exaggeration, my dear Sappho, religion…" Aunt Pátra begins. As he goes by, Peter flicks a little ball of bread between my thighs. "… my beauty," Aunt Pátra concludes, dabbing at her eyes.

Peter's eyes are laughing like the green marbles I stole from Zakoúlis yesterday, though farther down he's as serious as if he's at a funeral. Except for his gloves: they're shaking with laughter too. I permit my legs to laugh a little, then I bow my head into my plate and become good again.

"How do you see the situation, Sappho?" Mr. Stefanídes asks.

Grandmother is rolling her bread into little balls. "*Je suis trés pessimiste, mon cher.* Spine, *mon cher,* spine."

I know Grandmother well. She's crazy about politics. She detests artichokes and Communists. She loves the General very much and puts up with anchovies.

I love the General too. Every time he calls on us, he trots off to where his portrait is hanging (the one with the little holes in it) and, with his finger quivering at the row of medals, says:

"There I am," as though he's pointing to the spot where he's done his pipi.

"There you are," I sing back.

Second course: Canard a l'Orange. Wine: Chateauneuf-du-Pape.

I think of the lessons Peter's given me about the French wines and butchered cocks that Frenchmen eat with rotten fruit and olives, and I send him a kiss to show him I remember.

He serves me, his gloves catching in the pink ribbon stuck on my stomach.

"... so let's finally examine the problem *en face*," Mr. Aris concludes angrily, his face red as a radish, his mouth stuffed with food.

Mr. Aris talks so much he's like a book, which is why I always pay attention to him when he comes to the end, and then make up the beginning myself.

"*C'est une constipation*," Aunt Pátra says, fixing her hair.

"*Conspiration*, my dear Pátra, *conspiration*," Grandmother corrects, polite as a mirror.

Third course: Salade Niçoise. A dish of French cheeses. Wine: Chateau de la Ferroviere—"a good cork," I repeat to myself, remembering the lesson.

"Mr. Harílaos, try this Camembert. It's excellently ripe, sir."

Peter plonks a chunk on his plate, then goes down the

table and fills Aunt Pátra's glass to the brim. Standing back, he gazes at them both lovingly, like a Godmother.

"I'll tell you a dream I had," Uncle Harílaos announces, after finishing the game of chess he's been playing on the squares on the ceiling.

They all start chewing.

"You see, I have a stone in my garden, and I love it very much."

Uncle Harílaos is shining. Peter has stopped to listen, motionless as a dog. Uncle Harílaos' voice is like a mirror about to smash. I like it.

"... lots of stones, but I love this one more than any of the others—really don't know why."

I think of my red marble and I know exactly what Uncle Harílaos means.

"... I dreamed that one morning I took my stone, put it around my neck, and tied it fast so it wouldn't run away. Then I got on a bus for the sea. When I got there, I took a dive, sank right to the bottom, untied the stone, and started swimming around. A few years later I also married a Lady herring."

"A little Normandy butter with your cheese, dear?" Grandmother puts in. She is the perfect hostess.

Uncle Harílaos has nothing more to say, so he starts a game of chess on Mr. Stefanides' checkered suit.

Fourth course: Mousse au chocolat. Liqueur: Grand Marnier.

Peter serves me first because he knows how I like it. Bending, I touch him, my hands covered in chocolate. His legs are shaking a little as he turns to serve Grandmother, while I'm in a bit of a sweat from the Grand Marnier.

"… but to jump into bed with one—NEVER," Aunt Pátra shouts.

"Never, never more…" Uncle Harílaos murmurs.

"Red ones, black ones, yellow ones, green ones— aren't they all the same?" Bonnie asks.

"*Des gouts et des couleurs, n'est-ce pas?*" Aunt Pátra replies, delighted at her *jeux de mots*.

They all laugh and clap their hands, while Aunt Pátra swells out like a peacock.

"Cockadoodledoo!" I put in happily.

Uncle Harílaos is staring out of the window.

"Never, never more."

"Hush, Pátra, the child," Grandmother says, looking at me tenderly. I look back angelically.

Fifth course: Salade des fruits, with water from the faucet.

"I want to commit suicide, or at least just die, and play chess in Heaven with the new arrivals."

Peter leans heavily across Uncle Harílaos.

"A spot of liqueur, sir?"

"I would like to commit suicide, or at least just die, and—"

"Uncle Harílaos, hush now," I whisper, bending down and kissing his hand under the table.

Aunt Pátra's on her 15th glass, when Mr. Aris lights a cigar. I dive under the table. Peter's uniform jacket is long. Underneath the buttons are undone.

"A little salade des fruits, Mr. Aris?"

I grasp him.

"A little more wine, Madame?"

"A little cheese, sir?"

"A little salad?"

"My good man, I've told you already that I don't want any," I hear a voice say from way up.

"... and if Hitler had not lived..." someone high in the sky declares. Mr. Aris is turning into a book again, but I'm with Peter now.

"A little mousse, Miss?" Peter's voice is choked. The dish of mousse crashes down to the table.

"You've had a long day, Peter, my good man," Grandmother says coldly.

In the parlor, everybody sits on the settee and all around, waiting for Peter to bring in the coffee and cakes.

"Kassandra, my angel, have the chocolate one with chantilly."

"No, thanks, Grandmother, I'm absolutely bursting with mousse. But when Peter comes in, give it to him as a present from me. It's his birthday today, poor thing."

Next day, Uncle Harílaos committed suicide.

27. The Apple Falls From The Fig Tree

"General Inspection!" the General shouted when he came to our house one day.

He took me to my room, locked the door behind us, and when we came out again, my bottom and my ears hurt terribly, but I was pleased. The General had hung a medal on my dress. It was a picture of an apple with arms and legs embracing a fig tree. Above the apple's head there were gold letters that said:

"The Apple Falls From The Fig Tree."

I thanked the General, and when I went out in the afternoon for a walk, I threw myself at the trees, wrapped my arms around them and kissed them. A lot of people also gathered around and tried to bring me down from the top of an orange tree.

"The apple falls from the fig tree," I shouted to the passersby.

"But meatballs don't grow on orange trees," an old Lady shouted from below, and then some shiny Policemen came and took me home.

"Don't shout so loudly," they advised, "because there are enemies all around, who don't want apples to fall from the fig tree."

They gave me a medal too, but this one didn't have any gold letters. It was dumb, and I pinned it to my beret.

28. The Red Shoes

One night, I went to the movies with Grandmother. It was my first time and I was pleased. At the door, some pictures showed a Lady dancing on a grave.

"The film is called *The Red Shoes*," Grandmother said. She bought me a lollipop and the lights went out.

I stared at the pictures running on the wall all by themselves. A Lady had put on a pair of red shoes and wouldn't stop dancing. She couldn't take them off, neither could she stop dancing. Everything was so lovely that I had to grip my seat tightly so as not to start shouting. Meanwhile the Lady danced across yellow fields, jumped over hedges, danced from city to city—she couldn't take her shoes off, she cried and cried and danced till it was time for the movies to have an intermission.

I sat staring at the white wall, not daring to budge from my seat in case I missed the pictures. The lights went out and the Lady started dancing again.

"That's how all movies must be," I thought. "They must have the same Lady in the red shoes, running from movies to movies to dance. That's why they have an intermission: so she can make it from one to the other in time."

The Lady danced faster and faster. When she was old, she suddenly managed to take the shoes off. She lay down on a grave quite out of breath, and I just couldn't stop myself—I ran out to kiss her. I crashed into the wall, the Lady got scared and disappeared.

"Lady, Lady, don't get scared," I called. "Finish your dance and afterward come over to the house and dance over our walls as well."

But the lovely Lady had gone, and there was another picture on the wall. Rain was falling, large trees sang, and the red shoes sparkled all by themselves under the moon.

I was still there, stuck to the wall, when Grandmother grabbed me by the hair, the lights came on, and a little old Lady started selling peanuts and lollipops.

29. The Plasticine

"I," said my friend Hercules, "am going to become a Policeman when I grow up. I'm going to hide in corners, and whoever walks by whistling and pretending he doesn't care, I'm going to crack his head open."

"I," said I, "have quite made up my mind. I want to live with plasticine and tracings. I don't want to learn reading and writing. Fact is, I want to be plasticine. I'll take all my bones out and I'll knead myself."

Hercules closed his mouth. His Mother called the doctor, and Hercules wrote on a piece of paper that he'd never open it again, because if any air got in his belly, he'd turn into plasticine and I'd come and knead him.

"My dear Madame Sappho, I shall not be bringing him to your house again," Hercules' Mother said to Grandmother, "because ever since he started seeing your little girl, he's become a sleepwalker, he says that bats pencil their eyelashes, and that God works hand in hand with the Police and wears a corset. I hope you understand my position."

"I understand," said Grandmother.

"I understand," said I, and began seeing Zakoúlis.

30. National Festival

Last night, Grandmother took me to the National Stadium to see *The History of Greece*.

The people in the Stadium started clapping for Greece to appear on the platform, the lights went out, and a voice came out of the darkness, shouting:

"Long live the National Nation."

The lights went on, and I saw men in cloaks and moustaches coming on, holding hands and dancing the kalamatianós.*

"Those are the Ancients," Grandmother explained.

Then, more men in cloaks came on, only this time they had beards and no moustaches.

"Those are the Christians."

In the middle came the Ladies, doing somersaults and singing "A Brave Greek Airman I'll Become."

I liked everything very much. It reminded me of the circus.

"Oh, Grandmother, I've never seen Greece like this before, with so many colors and so many acrobats. Oh, Grandmother, I've never seen her with her hair down and without a hat. Where's she been hiding all this time? Oh, my darling little Greecey, my little Greecey-weecey!" I kept on screeching for a long time, till *The History of Greece* ended, and Greece went off to bed, and we returned home.

* Popular Greek folk dance. *Trans.*

31. The House with the Rooms

One afternoon, Mother and Father and several other Gentlemen looked at me and wept.

"We'll take you to a lovely house with rooms," Mother said. "You'll be inside, and we'll be outside. There'll be lawns, and every morning some Gentlemen will come to see you, and they'll stare at you. Then in the afternoon, you'll go out for a walk all around and ring bells in your room to call fat Ladies in. We on the outside will come inside to talk to you. You'll be eating foamy cakes too."

"Thank you kindly," I said, rubbing my eyeballs.

On Thursday, Mother and Father took me to a lovely house in the middle of lawns and full of rooms. Gentlemen in short trousers were leaping up and down in the park, sticking their tongues out to get some fresh air.

A few years later, I went down in the park to play with the Gentlemen. In the evenings we also played games and laughed as much as we liked. It was nice.

One day, while we were playing on the table, a Lady grabbed me by the hair.

"Why did you call me a kipper?" she yelled.

She grabbed my nose as well, tried to tear it out and take it with her. I was upset because I hadn't said a thing to her, and in fact I'd been patting her head.

"I'll slaughter you," the Lady screamed. "I'll come after dark and pull your jaws out."

A Gentleman rushed in and grabbed the Lady who'd grabbed me.

On Sunday, Mother and etcetera came to talk to me. When I told them about it, we laughed a lot, then we ran off to go boating on the little lake.

One day, in the house, I was introduced to Monsieur Clovis. He was in the house as well and thought he was a Mademoiselle. He had a bucket too, and made patisseries in the sandpit in the park. We talked awhile and he fixed my hair in a bun.

We became good friends and I taught him how to pencil his eyebrows.

One day Monsieur Clovis got angry.

"He's very dangerous," Monsieur Jacques told me confidentially.

"You're very dangerous, Monsieur Clovis," I told him.

He bit my arm and blood seeped out, thick and perfumed. Then we became friends again.

Since then, many years went by. One day, Mother came in the car to take me from the house and drive me to our house. As we were pulling away, with my arm thrown out of the window, I waved goodbye to my friends, the Gentlemen and Ladies, who were also moving their arms there and here.

32. The Prince and the Pauper

Aunt Pátra came to tell me a story.

"Today I'll tell you *The Prince and the Pauper*."

She brought out a bottle with yellow juice from her handbag, took a gulp, and hid it under my bed.

"Once upon a time, there was a Prince who had the same kind of yellow hair as a Pauper, so he said to him: 'Shall we swap? You'll become the Prince for a while, and I'll become the Pauper. I'm fed up in here, I want to go out for a walk, just like Paupers do,' he said. 'OK by me,' said the Pauper, who put on the gold uniform and walked right into the Palace—"

"But, Aunt Pátra, I want to hear about the walk the Prince took. I'm fed up with the Palace."

But Aunt Pátra was worried about the Pauper.

"Oh, my God, how will he ever be able to wash his hands in rose water? How will he manage to speak politely? How will he know how to eat like a Gentleman?"

Aunt Pátra was in a sweat and she was breathing hard, so she dived under the bed, grabbed her bottle, and drank it all up. Soiled her dress too.

"This story upsets me terribly, sweetie."

Her eyes went marble, she began to hiccup.

I broke out in a sweat too and sang along with Aunt Pátra:

O my God,
How will he speak politely?
How will he eat like a Gentleman?

How will he wash with rose water?

Aunt Pátra tried to get up, but fell flat on the floor and started snoring. I burst into tears.

"Aunt Pátra, stop it. I can't stand it."

Then I played with my dolls.

That night, when I went to bed, I kept becoming the Prince, then the Pauper, then the Prince again. The Prince would get lost in the forest, the peasants would find him and give him something to eat, but he'd eat so prettily that the peasants would tell who he was immediately and when he'd ask for some rose water, they'd chop off his head.

In the Palace, the Pauper would be very polite. Nobody would find him out, but as soon as they'd bring him something to eat, he'd smear himself with sauce and drink the rose water, and they'd hang him.

I turned over on my left side and became the Prince, then on my right side and became the Pauper. I got out of bed, stood before the mirror, and became both at once. Every time I got to the rose water, I burst into tears.

In the morning, I put on some rags I found in the attic and went for a walk to the kitchen.

"Come and have your breakfast," Faní said, collaring me.

"Faní, dear Faní, darling," I yelled, "don't chop my head off!"

The house was in uproar. Grandmother came rushing down too.

"What are you doing to the child?" she said, collaring Faní and slapping her. "What is the meaning of these rags?" she said to me. "Go up to your room immediately and put on something decent."

I went up and put on my blue dress with the crescent moons and returned to the dining room for breakfast. Grandmother rang the bell and Peter brought in the breakfast. I saw the rose water beside Grandmother's plate.

"Don't hang me, please! Don't hang me!" I shouted.

I dashed down to the kitchen, came back with the clothesline, and gave it to Grandmother.

"Here, Grandmother dear, let's get it over with," I said, closing my eyes.

33. The Kitten

I wanted an animal. Dolls didn't speak, they weren't warm, they didn't breathe, nor did they love me. Or lick me. I wanted an animal, to love me, and I'd love it back. I wanted a kitten. I'd put it right next to me and look at it. It would be mine. I'd give it a name and it would know mine.

At night, in bed, I thought about it: a kitten, round like an egg, sleeping at my feet, keeping me warm while I kept it warm.

I told Grandmother, Friday.

"No, it'll mess up the house. It'll pipi in the parlor and poopoo on the armchairs and scratch them."

"Grandmother, I want a kitten."

"No!"

"Grandmother, a kitten, I want one. Grandmother, I want a kitten."

"No!"

She'd pay for this.

In the morning, when I woke up, Saturday, I got some evaporated milk and poured it all over the house. Then I did poopoo in front of the fireplace and pipi on the Empire settee. They were so disgusted that nobody scolded me.

Next day, Sunday, a kitten, yellow like honey, was waiting for me in the dining room. Trembling with love, I took him on my knees and stayed like that till evening.

"I only brought it for a week," Grandmother said, Sunday. "It's borrowed."

I'd never give him back. I'd rather kill him first.

It was the first time I felt *happy*, as the grown-ups called it in the parlor. I bought a basket for him and became his Mother. Then I christened him Borrowedy, and he called me Mother. I took him for walks in my doll's carriage, and when the sun was hot, I raised the hood to shield his head. He didn't mess the house even once, but always did his pipi in a box I'd painted gold with silver stripes.

I felt like a Mother. Sometimes, milk ran from my breasts and I melted with sweetness. I didn't see anybody anymore. The days with Borrowedy passed like sugar, it was Thursday. The days with Borrowedy passed like whipped cream, it was Friday. There was such a smile splitting my mouth that it was impossible for me to close it. At night he slept in my sheets, on my belly.

"I love you," I told him, before I said my prayers. He purred, and my belly sweated with his love.

"On Sunday I'll be giving it back," Grandmother said. "Sunday I gave it to you, and Sunday I'll be taking it back."

The week was ending.

"Darling Borrowedy," I lullabied him like a baby.

I started next day, Saturday. First I beat him a lot. He didn't cry, just stared at me and purred. He thought I was petting him. I got clothespins and pinned them to his ears like earrings. He stared at me, knowing how much I loved him. Between kicks, I cried and kissed him.

I grabbed him by the tail and spun him around and around, like the horses on the merry-go-round. He didn't howl, just stared at me and purred. In the evening I tossed him slowly and rhythmically at the wall. His back broke and he dragged himself to my knees, purring.

Next day, Sunday, I hung him head down and stuck needles in his eyes.

"Borrowedy," I kept telling him, "my darling Borrowedy."

In the afternoon, I filled the bath and held him under for a long time. He beat his legs against the tub so he could come up and breathe. Yellow juices ran from his eyes.

When it wasn't moving anymore, I put it in its basket, covered it with its little pink blanket, and took it to Grandmother.

I left it in the dining room.

Sunday evening.

34. The Picnic

One afternoon we went on a picnic to the seaside in Uncle Harílaos' car.

When we got to the beach, we spread the tablecloth with the flowers on the sand and put all the food out on it. Aunt Pátra stuck her cane in the chicken, and Grandmother took *Brothers Karamazov* from her bag and started reading.

"Shall we go for a walk?" Uncle Harílaos said, taking me by the hand, and we ran off to the water's edge.

"Kassandra, tell me the story of the mermaid."

Uncle Harílaos was staring at the sea as though he wanted to drink it up. We sat on a rock.

"All right. There's a mermaid, you see, who calls me when it gets dark. Her legs are nailed to the bottom of the sea, and she's so tall her head touches Heaven. Fish swim in her eyes and flowers grow in them—you know, Uncle Harílaos, at the bottom of the sea everything's green, and when you raise your head, you see a new sky, all wet and wavy."

Uncle Harílaos looked at Grandmother and Aunt Pátra motionless on the sand, then he turned to stare at the water again.

"Tell me another."

"Uncle Harílaos, we must be getting back. Grandmother's finishing her chapter."

I pulled him by the hand, but his trousers had got all tangled in the seaweed. If I'd let go of him, he would have quite turned into a fish and Aunt Pátra would have got very cross.

Just then it started to rain. Grandmother opened her umbrella.

"I'll sit next to the sardines to keep an eye on them," Uncle Harílaos whispered to me so that Aunt Pátra wouldn't hear. "In case they smell the sea, you know, and take off."

"Don't worry, Uncle Harílaos, I'll keep an eye on them too."

Uncle Harílaos stretched out on the sand beside the sardines. The drops rolled down his cheeks and his hat became a pond. Grandmother was starting on her second chapter, and Aunt Pátra, her finger stabbed at the sky, was giving the rain a thorough telling off.

35. We're All the Same

I dropped in to see the General. I had my rod and line with me because I was planning to do a spot of fishing afterward.

I was shown into the parlor. The General was wearing his uniform jacket with the medals over his pajamas, and he had tied his wife to a chair.

"Kassandra, my dear," the General said, "she's been reading thick books of late and today she told me: 'Tryphon, we're all the same. One day we're all going to die.' So I grabbed her on the spot and tied her to the chair and began the interrogation."

"Ah, my dear General, allow me to ask Aunt Samantha a few questions myself. I'll do something that will make her tell us everything."

I started tickling the soles of Aunt Samantha's feet.

"Speak! Speak!" the General shouted.

"*Gone with the Wind,*" Aunt Samantha screamed.

"More, more!" the General shouted.

"My dear General, would you do me a favor? Would you allow me to tie you up as well? I'd like to try something new, and if I succeed, Aunt Samantha will tell us everything."

I tied the General up (he helped me too), having sat down next to Aunt Samantha, and brought my rod and line from the hall.

"Now I'm going to fish for information," I explained to him, taking a little shrimp from my satchel and sticking it on my hook.

"Untie me, untie me!" the General shouted, but I was enjoying myself.

I cast the line and the little shrimp went up his nostril; I tickled Aunt Samantha's feet and also fished her wig.

Then I put my rod on my shoulder.

"I'm off to catch a few fish now. I'll be back tomorrow."

I also put the painting of The General On His White Horse on the table, in front of them, so they wouldn't get bored.

36. Alberto

It happened when I was taken ill and kept seeing butter-flies and swallows. I saw crabs and spiders too, crocodiles and poppies.

The plants in the house moved about, they fluttered at the windows. The passionflower wrapped itself around itself, coloring the walls green as it danced.

I filled the bathtub and curled up in it, caressing the water all around. I liked it because my self would leap out of me and chase me all over the ceiling.

All of a sudden, I found myself in the street.

"Which way are you heading, Miss?"

A big bird (car) had stopped in front of me.

"Could I drop you somewhere?"

The bird was flying very fast, and panting, and I was in it too.

"My name is Alberto. And yours?" the Gentleman with the bird asked.

The sky around was black and thick.

The Gentleman's bed was soft, like meat against my body, which was now naked. A suction pipe was sucking out my belly and licking up my blood. The Gentleman was licking the bath water off my legs and the soles of my feet. I was boiling. The Gentleman was licking my belly, and in my belly where the Gentleman was licking, crabs raced around and jellyfish floated about.

With my left hand I crushed a fly on the bald head of Mr. Alberto, who was rolling me and squeezing me and sucking me like a cupping glass, all of him inside and on top and below.

Under the meat of the bed, the Gentlemen's juices trickled and the butterflies fluttered serenely. I grasped Mr. Alberto's front part, which was thick and reminded me of relay races at school.

Stuff dripped from his nails, and all of a sudden I found myself elsewhere again.

"Could I drop you at your house, Miss?"

"Yes, thank you kindly," I said, twining my fingers and shivering.

The swallows were waiting in the corridor.

37. The Party with the Greek Philosopher

I'm in Paris to see Mother, and this afternoon I'm having a *bal masqué*.

All my girl friends are coming to my party; we haven't invited any boys because they bore us.

Mother's been bored since morning. Grandmother and Grandfather have gone off to Baden-Baden to take the waters, and Grandmother has given Peter leave. As usual, he's gone off to Le Touquet to play at the casino.

Therefore, Mother has had to stay alone, and now she's moaning and groaning as she fries the meatballs.

"And I had a trip to go on," she snaps.

"And I had to see a friend," she sniffs.

Her face brightens.

"I'll call up my friend the Philosopher to be your Governess this afternoon. He's a Marxist too!"

Together they turn the house into a Children's House. There are streamers everywhere, magic lanterns, and jellies like colored fishes. The house is a Children's House from the parquet to the ceiling.

I dress up as a Devil: black tights up to my neck, black velvet horns, and a bushy black tail with a hole at the tip for the flames to come out. I'm bursting with devilishness.

The girls arrive, all of them clutching their dolls. We begin by playing games: hide-and-seek, musical chairs, postman's knock.

"Now why don't you take a break, Kassandra, my dear?" the Philosopher tells Mother. "Go out for a while."

"Will you look after them?" Mother asks.

"Of course I will," the Marxist says.

Mother hesitates a moment, then puts on her coat and leaves, shattered by so much childhoodness.

"Let's play Wolf, Wolf, Are You Here?" the Philosopher suggests, switching off the lights, and we run off to hide.

"Wolf, wolf, are you here?" we all sing out together.

"I'm putting on my specs to see you better."

"Wolf, wolf, are you here?"

"I'm putting on my dentures to eat you better."

"He forgot to do Grandmother in bed," Laure says, sighing behind the curtain. "He's cheating."

Edwige pipies in her panties. Like a good hostess I switch on the lights.

"Philosopher, we don't like this game."

We put our dolls to sleep on the bed, so they won't get tired with all the fuss going on, and cover them with a blanket.

"MAMA!" their bellies whimper, and they fall asleep.

The Marxist arranges us nicely in a circle. We sit cross-legged and happy on the floor, while he remains standing, holding a little red ball.

"Let's play syllables. I'll toss you the ball that's one syllable. You toss it back—that's another syllable, and so on. This way we'll make pretty little wordies."

He tosses the ball to Laure.

"Ma-"

"Ma," Laure shouts, tossing the ball back proudly.

He tosses the ball to Mouchette.

"So-"

"Sage," Mouchette shouts back.

To Melusine.

"Sir-"

"Vant," Melusine shouts, kissing the ball and sending it back.

The Philosopher catches it and bites it at the spot where Melusine kissed it.

To Edwige.

"Pee-"

"Nut."

The Marxist misses the ball and it falls in the orange juice. He fishes it out and licks it dry.

My turn. I fix my tail.

"Ass-"

"End," I shout.

He tosses it back.

"Nic," I shout.

He tosses it back.

"Ass-"

I lob it back to him naked, without a word.

He tosses it back.

"Ass-"

I toss it up to the ceiling, he catches it and kisses it. Then he tosses it back.

"Ass-"

"HOLE!" I shout, shoving the little red ball in my mouth and sucking it.

The Philosopher's trousers swell like a little cloud.

He tosses the ball to Laure.

"Pee-"

"Ple," Laure shouts.

He tosses it back.

"Pee-"

"Soup." Laure's eyes fill.

"Pee-"

"HOLE!" Laure screams and dives under the bed.

"And now children, we'll play another game. Whoever I toss the ball to will come and give me a wee little kiss."

We clap happily.

The ball falls under Mouchette's skirt. She plonks a kiss on his cheek.

We clap happily.

The ball falls on Melusine's lap. She kisses the Marxist on the right tip of his moustache.

We clap happily.

The ball falls inside Edwige's blouse. The Philosopher puts his hand in casually, and when he pulls it out again, Edwige dives under the table.

We clap happily.

The ball falls between my legs. The Philosopher kneels and takes my cheeks in his hands. A tongue licks my eyebrows, nose, and neck, trembles around my mouth, dives down my throat, caresses my belly, and comes out through the soles of my feet.

We clap happily.

"And now, children, we'll try another game. One of you will toss me the ball and order me to do things."

Edwige: "Philosopher, lift your arm up."

Melusine: "Philosopher, do a somersault."

Laure: "Philosopher, grind your teeth."
Me: "Marxist, pull your pants down."
We clap happily.
We all sing together, keeping time.

Pull your pants down
down down down
pull your pants down
down down down.

The Philosopher comes up to me, tears my tail off, and I lose my devilishness. The jelly overflows, spills all over the parquet. The Marxist stands with my tail wrapped around his legs.

He unbuttons his pants, licking the ball. He drops his pants and stands there with a white cloth around him, just like a baby. He drops the cloth. He wraps my tail around him, making it a snake and putting the tip with the flames in his mouth.

We all stare at this huge, dense, dumb thing, something like an eggplant left out in the sun. Between 2 little red balls.

Edwige and Melusine rush to hide behind the armchair. Laure and Mouchette grab their dolls and dive under the bed. France and Clea hide in the bathtub, after first turning the faucets on. I stare at him for a long time, then put my head between my legs and become an ostrich.

The Marxist pulls his pants up and leaves, whistling.

And here comes Mother. We scramble out of hiding. She finds us stuck to each other like a bunch of grapes, playing snakes and ladders.

"Have you had a good time, children?"
Not a squeak.
"How was the party, Kassandra?"
Mother stares at me, I stare at my tights.
"Mother, I've lost my tail."

38. The Marbles

I'm in my room. Since yesterday, it's been winter. I've arranged my dolls in line on the bed, opened their legs, and lifted their frocks. I'm making them give birth. I'm using my marbles—the shiny ones—a present from Peter.

The marbles drop, and roll on the carpet. After they've turned into children, I put them in my basket. It's the birth basket. It's very shiny, with bits of mirror inside, 1 gold penknife, and millions of marbles—red ones, yellow ones, green ones—fire.

I want to put marbles in my dolls' bellies so I prick them all with a needle. They sigh, as straw falls on the carpet, and look pleased. I close their legs, cover them up, and run off to see the rain.

I open the window and turn the light off. Drops fill the room, the whole room sings with drops, fills with shining children, and I put my basket under the sky. Steel drops joggle with the marbles. I sit at the window and put the basket on my lap to sing the rain.

The room fills with green, yellow, red rains.

Someone knocks.

"Mother," I say aloud, shutting my eyes.

I don't know who it is out there, neither do I know what the word means, but I know that when the door opens, I'll understand.

Someone is in the room. Now I shall *see* the word *Mother*. I chant my magic things, squeeze the word *Mother* in my belly, and look.

I see Peter, smiling.

He kneels, shoves his nose inside my dolls, and sniffs at them, feeling for the holes with his tongue. Then, taking off his shirt, he stands at the window. His hairs turn yellow, red, green—fire—he's covered in flashing rains, he blazes up to the ceiling, opening his mouth and swallowing the round, shiny drops.

I close my eyes and hear him drop brand-new marbles in my basket.

39. A Visit to the Gentleman with the So's and the Questions

I stammer a lot. By the time I can bring out a word, it gets dark; sometimes the sun rises before I can get it out. It doesn't matter. Except that I'll be going to school in the autumn, which upsets Grandmother so much that she swells out like a peacock.

"Say it, my child," she prompts. "Say it," she insists, her voice going hoarse.

She's concerned about school a lot.

"How will you ever be able to answer, my child, when they ask you about the rivers and mountain chains?"

Not a squeak.

At table: "Are you hungry? Would you like an artichoke?"

Grandfather: "Is she stupid or something?"

My head shapes a NO like an egg.

In the last few days, I've gone completely dumb. The words scratch my throat like shoes. I bleed. Nothing comes out—except a grunt now and then, when I'm hungry.

"Grrrrrr," I go, and they bring me some spinach.

If only I knew how to write.

The Family holds a council to discuss my speech.

"Now we've got a new headache, Pátra, my dear," Grandmother tells Aunt Pátra. "The child is not doing very well at all with her speech."

"*Alpha, Beta, Gamma*," Grandfather mouths thoughtfully.

It's only now and then with Miss Benbridge that a word escapes from me by mistake. In English the words are sweeter, more swollen; they're like gargling, they scratch less. And besides, Miss Benbridge is not a member of the Family.

At table, in English: "Are you hungry?"

In the evening: "Are you sleepy?"

In the afternoon: "You filthy little brat."

Me, in English: "Mmmmmiss Benbridge, you're llllike a pppppottttato."

The Family celebrates.

Today the house is buzzing with activity. This afternoon, Grandmother is having a tea party for *un groupe des Dames* from her Good Works (the Department for the Mongoloids). I'm supposed to recite "The Little Blue Angel Looks at Me and Smiles from Above" in English. There are 10 stanzas to it, and by the time I'm through, the tea and toast will be stone cold.

"Oh, that child." Grandmother's dentures creak—and they're brand-new ones too.

When I'm alone, I talk endlessly: to my dolls (lessons in *bonnes manières*), at the walls and doors—nothing can stop me. I become a toilet flush, a Niagara Falls, a running nose, puke. With the Family around, the words shrivel, become round and heavy like stones, fall deep inside me, impossible to fish out again.

This morning I've put on my best clothes: the patent-leather shoes with the green toes, the frock with the crescent moons, and the white sailor cap.

"I'm taking you to a Gentleman," Grandmother

informs me. "You'll eat candies, and he'll teach you to speak."

A Lady asks us to take a seat, gazing at us like a Grandmother.

"Mr. Frídas will receive you immediately."

"Grrrrrr," I go, and Grandmother licks her nails and sighs.

"Come in," a tall, kind, serious Gentleman says. "I'll see the child alone."

Grandmother crosses her legs, opens the *Brothers Karamazov,* and lights a cigarette.

The Gentleman takes me to an armchair and sits himself behind a desk—to keep a distance. He stares at me. I stare at him. I hear the clock behind my head: tic-toc-tic-toc-tic-toc.

"Tic-toc, sir," I say shyly.

"So," he replies, "it appears you don't want to speak to us."

"It depends, sir. In fact, my tongue just won't stop. I don't know where to put it. When I stuff it in my pocket, it talks. When I hide it in my cap, it sings. I just don't know what to do to stop it."

Mr. Frídas stares at me.

"My child, why don't you talk to your Relations?"

"But I do talk to them, only I don't use words."

"Imagine I'm your Mother."

"With the breasts you have I wouldn't mind having you as my Nanny, sucking away at you and bursting with yogurt and evaporated milk. I like it around here. You've got lots of books full of words, a fantastic little settee, and an armchair that's just like a nest. Mr. Frídas, I love you very much."

"Would you like to talk to me again tomorrow?"

"We can talk as much as you like. Tomorow I'll tell you the story of the Lady dancer. The first night she danced, the Opera caught fire. Firemen, water, the lot— oh, it was a mess. And here's another story: a nun escaped from the convent of St. Efpraxía and decided to get married. But she loved money too much. When she married the richest man in the world, she just couldn't stop herself and she was very soon stealing from him. To be continued tomorrow."

"That'll be all for today," the Gentleman says.

"How was the visit?" Grandmother asks.

Not a squeak.

From now on I'll talk only to Mr. Frídas.

40. St. Sebastian

Grandmother is cross-stitching black wings on her swans. I'm gazing at the fire. Miss Benbridge is arriving today.

Whenever a new Governess arrives, Grandmother addresses her severely, asks her for a bunch of papers, and then offers her tea. Some stay for a short time, but others leave almost as soon as they step into the parlor, and that's because I take one look at their shoes and ankles, and if I don't like what I see, I make a rush at them and bite their ankles or shoes, and they leave right away.

"Bite them all," Peter tells me, after I've bitten the first 10 this winter, so I've stayed without a Governess for months and months. I've had Peter for a Nanny, and we've had a nice time.

Last night he dressed up as a Governess: a frock, stockings, pointy shoes, he put rouge on his cheeks, and we went out for a walk. Nobody guessed a thing. When it got dark, we went to a house where other Peters had dressed up as Governesses and Ladies too.

We were shown into the parlor, and there, all the other Peters started grabbing Peter's breasts, and I grabbed everybody's breasts. I wished I'd had them all as Governesses, and I hoped that perhaps my next Governess, at least, would be a friend of Peter's and that Grandmother would not guess a thing, and the 3 of us would stay together, and at night go for a walk and find the others.

The parlor was red, and Saints in gold frames hung on the walls. I'd never seen so many Saints all together.

Their eyes were turned to the sky, their hair waved yellow on the black walls, the Peters tapped with their fans the red moles they'd sewn on their necks, and Peter knelt and kissed the crescent moons on my frock.

"I have the honor of presenting my Queen to you!"

They all fell into line for the introductions; they became a shining snake.

"Miss Bianca, Duchess of Montenegro."

I curtsied, went on.

"Miss Samantha-My-Mother-Has-Died."

"You have a nice title, Miss. Has she been dead long?"

"She died today, dear."

She laughed, her gold teeth blinding me, and I went on, down the line.

"Miss Svenda, Princess of the Frozen Seas."

"Madam, however Frozen you may be, you are boiling in your lace."

Miss Svenda's mouth drooped like a stalactite—

"Simmering," I added quickly, and she smiled.

"Miss Belinda Ballerina. I dance battles, hurricanes, and the Bible to myself."

She jumped in the air, and I jumped too out of politeness.

"Miss Georgette."

"Don't you have a title, Miss?"

She showed me her white neck.

"I understand, Miss Georgette. What need have you of titles, when you are so beautiful that you shimmer like a fish." Peter tossed her a gardenia.

"My little cabbage, what would I do without you?" he whispered.

I lifted my frock, I became the sky, and the crescent moons filled out.

"The Queen of Peter!" I called out.

The snake fell to its knees.

"Dear Ladies, when I grow up, I too want to become good like a Saint and beautiful like a Gentleman."

They liked this very much and they all started touching me. They smelled of incense and jasmine.

"Oh, Grandmother, how proud you'd be of me now," I thought.

"I shall dance the Death of the Swan for you," Miss Belinda shouted, but nobody was listening.

"Miss Belinda Ballerina, please dance it for me," I said, sitting on the floor.

Miss Belinda Ballerina jumped in the air and tossed her gloves to me, her diamond necklace and her black curls. She tossed me her frock too, and she fell at my feet, pretending she was fluttering her wings for the last time. He was so beautiful in his lace and shaven head that I bent down and kissed his long eyelashes. Afterward I ran to Peter and climbed on his knees.

"Peter, look at Miss Georgette, I like her more than all the others."

"Me too." Peter's eyes became copper.

"Would you like me to show you around?"

I took the arm of Miss Bianca, Duchess of Montenegro. Black hairs jumped out of the muslin.

"I am making a collection of Saints, my dear, Pre-Raphaelites."

"And I, Miss Bianca, am making a collection of

marbles. Pre-Grandmothers."

We stopped all of a sudden.

"And there is St. Sebastian, my favorite."

He was so beautiful I could have fainted. He was all covered in blood, and his blue eyes gazed tearfully at a little cloud.

"Why have you cut the picture in two?" I asked. Even the little cloud was in half.

"Ah, my dear, I can't bear seeing those Evil Ones firing their arrows into him."

She was crying, though I couldn't see any Evil Ones anywhere. She stepped on my foot and this alarmed me.

"But the arrows don't hurt him, you know. He's bleeding because of his own beauty."

Miss Bianca was by now jumping up and down on my shoe. I had to say something.

"But, Miss Bianca, if *I* myself feel like crying about it, how much more must he cry when he's so beautiful?" I said bursting into tears as well.

"The Evil Ones, the Evil Ones, they're to blame for everything."

She clung to me and we wept together, jumping up and down.

"Miss Bianca, Miss Bianca, stop now. The arrows make him even more beautiful. Would he ever have had such eyes if he didn't hurt anywhere?"

This comforted her, so she smiled sadly at her Saint and disappeared.

I frowned: "St. Sebastian, aren't you ashamed of yourself? How can you bear to make the Ladies cry like this?"

He winked at me, then hurriedly turned his gaze back at the little cloud.

I ran off to find the others.

"Let me show you how to play the game Are You A Governess Or Aren't You?" I shouted.

I won. The only real Governess was me.

"Miss Bianca," I said, "as my prize I want The-Other-Half-Of-St.-Sebastian-With-The-Evil-Ones."

She brought it to me nicely rolled up, and in order to please her I stood on the table and sang "10 Little Indian Boys," then we blew out the candles and played Wolf, Wolf, Are You Here? I saw Peter approach Miss Georgette. He looked scared, like Little Red Riding Hood approaching the Wolf and begging him to swallow her down, and she's dressed in red on purpose so he can recognize her—and they fell behind the settee together.

A waltz was on the record player and, in the dark, I was dancing about on my own. I stepped on an eyelash, St. Sebastian was laughing and smelled of sweat, the Saints were all holding hands and singing hymns, their feet dripping fire, fire shooting from their mouths, and, taking off, I swam up to the ceiling. From high up there the room looked like a field, and the Peters in each other's arms like a little hill of tulips.

Feeling very sleepy, I took a high dive and came down again, climbed onto a Gentleman and fell asleep in his frock. The little hill of Peters danced slowly, lullabying me. Then Peter picked me up in his arms and tiptoed out. The sun had come up.

This morning I woke up in bed and ran off to

Grandmother to tell her the nice dream I'd had, but then I remembered that Grandmother had forbidden me to dream the dreams I like, so I'm keeping it secret.

Grandmother's stitching black wings on her swans and I'm gazing at the fire.

"Oh, Miss Benbridge," I say to myself, "how I would love you to be a friend of Peter's, and especially a Scotsman dressed up as my Governess. Don't be afraid, I'll be the only one to know about it. I'll be able to tell who you are by your curls and painted mouth."

The door opens and the ugliest shoes I've ever seen enter. I attack. I get a kick that knocks me over on the carpet on my back. I attack again and get another kick.

"What are the things you like to eat, my child?" she asks.

I tell her all the things I like, chanting them in turn, like a poem.

"From now on you'll eat only artichokes."

"Miss Benbridge, would you like your tea with lemon or milk?" Grandmother asks, rubbing her hands.

I race to my room and hide under the bed. And right there, under the bed, I see a painting. It's The-Other-Half-Of-St.-Sebastian-With-The-Evil-Ones. I hug it and whisper to the soldiers:

"If you go and kill Miss Benbridge, I promise you the next time I go to Miss Bianca's I'll bring you St. Sebastian himself."

The soldiers laugh and ask me for a mirror. They comb their hair in the mirror, then raise their bows.

41. The House Boat

My Mother, Kassandra, sent me a letter:

My Dear Kassandra,

I dreamed that we were taking a walk on a boat, but it wasn't a boat—it was like a house and the water was like the earth. The walls were tall, and the doors long and narrow. Everything was light; we could turn everything into something else whenever we liked.

We did this often. When we saw a hill or a bit of earth or a bridge, we knocked down a door or twisted it around or threw it in the water, and the houseboat sailed on. Nothing could stop it. It slid over the waves and I felt as though I was sliding inside me too. I felt I was at the bottom of the sea.

So we took doors off their hinges, took walls down and changed them over, we passed through caves and saw the sun fall in the sea and disappear.

When it got dark, I gathered stars and scattered them in the water. Then I stood on the tips of my toes, took down the moon, and hung it around your neck.

Kassandra

42. Grandfather Goes to Nursery School

Grandfather still goes to nursery school. He wears short trousers and does his additions with yellow beads.

Every morning, Grandmother gets his schoolbag ready for him, putting in a sandwich and a chocolate. Saturdays she puts in a stick of chewing gum as well. I haven't started going to nursery school yet, so when Grandfather comes home, he tells me all about it. They don't play with him much in the playground because he punches everyone and won't let them use the trampoline.

Grandfather's been at nursery school for many years. Grandmother goes to the Parents' Meetings, where the teacher talks about the children and gives advice. She told Grandmother that sometimes Grandfather comes to class without having done his homework.

"Niónios, if you don't draw the house with the chimney for your teacher, I won't take you out for a walk tomorrow," Grandmother warns him. Grandfather bursts into tears, stamps his foot on the floor, and Grandmother takes down his pants and gives him a good spanking.

Yesterday, we went to the end-of-the-year school show. The children played *The Birth of Jesus*, and Grandfather was one of the sheep that keep the baby warm. It was very nice.

Later they gave out the school report cards, then all of us ran to the playground, where we played cops and robbers. In the evening, when we got home, Grandfather was not feeling well and was sent straight to bed. He had mumps, which made him very upset, because he was going to miss nursery school, not so much for the lessons—as he explained to me—but for recess.

43. That Afternoon a Bee Had Stung Her

"Does it hurt, Mother?"

That afternoon a bee had stung her under her nightgown, on her belly.

Autumn had come. Elsewhere, the leaves must have been falling from the trees, the sun sad, the earth getting ready to sleep again. Here, on the bare island, only the sea had gone darker; it had become bad.

"Does it hurt, Mother?"

She took off her nightgown, went to the bottom of the garden, sat on a rock, naked, facing the sunset, and rubbed her swollen belly. She gazed out to sea.

"Does it hurt, Mother?"

A lizard scurried into my bathing suit.

The sun poured over the sea like ink, the garden of our house was ablaze. Autumn had come, and we were alone on the island: Mother, Minos, and I.

Minos was a Father to me. He lifted me up on his shoulders and ran deep into the sea, which was good to me, with me clinging to the back of his head and laughing, because he was strong and good, and he was a man, with legs and arms. Then we'd come home all covered in salt, Minos would close the wooden shutters and stretch out in the cool sheets, his eyes open, waiting for night to fall. Mother would stretch out beside him, and she would tend him like a mermaid. I'd run off to chase lizards.

Autumn had come; only *our* house was still alive.

Elsewhere, children must have started school, with schoolbags and sharp pencils, with angry and kind teachers.

The sun didn't burn anymore, it went away early. I was afraid of the sea now. As soon as I touched it, it licked me, kissed me, ready to suck me down. I couldn't see the bottom anymore. At noon the sky clouded over. It was as if the sea was giving birth to autumn monsters in the depths, and hiding them down there. Its color got darker and darker, its waves went dumb, huge. In the last few days it had become carnivorous too.

Minos didn't lift me up on his shoulders anymore, but took me by the hand instead, and we ran along the beach, stopping every now and then and looking at the water and shivering. When night fell, he caressed my hair and kissed me.

Yesterday, a wave like a mountain stopped at the window of my room. It slid along the pane, caressing itself, coaxing me to let it in.

"I must be dreaming," I thought.

I was.

The wave looked at me, laughing. If I'd opened the pane, it would have swallowed me down, wandered about with me far and wide, taken me down to the depths, and there it would have forgotten me.

I got scared. The dream was for real. I got so scared I opened the door. Mother was standing there, laughing.

"Come!"

We both bent over Minos, who was sleeping, his fists tight like a baby. She took off her nightgown, became a bird on him, an octopus, arms and legs around him, her eyes on me.

Next day, we went for a walk, Minos and I. He was crying.

"You're my daughter," he said thoughtfully, hopefully.

"You're my Father."

He was crying.

The sun was very red, filling his face with such light that I shut my eyes so as not to be blinded. I loved him so much I would have liked to turn him into a statue, kiss his feet, light fires around him, and worship him.

On the way home, the beach was covered in seaweed—I almost choked with the smell—the house had gone green, it had become sea-like.

"Minos!"

I became a seashell in his arms, our tears and mouths became sea-like too.

"Minos!"

"Goodbye," Minos said.

Mother was in the garden in her nightgown. She'd opened her legs to suck up the last rays of the sun, when a bee had stung her under her nightgown, on her belly. Her face became a sting.

"Does it hurt, Mother?"

Taking off her nightgown, she rubbed her swollen belly. Then she went to the bottom of the garden, sat on a rock, naked, facing the sunset. She gazed out to sea. Her eyes filled with seaweed.

Night.

"Come!"

She took me by the hand. We bent over Minos, who was sleeping like a baby.

"Dance!"

I knew Minos was going to die.

I danced. With my arms stretched out before me, I became a woman. In my hands I held a tray, which I was going to pile high with heads she would eat for dessert. I danced rhythmically, in a circle, sea-like, around Minos, who was naked as a baby. I took my bathing suit off and stayed without a skin.

"Caress him!"

Her command filled me and I took hold of Minos' strength, which swelled as it gazed up at the ceiling, crying, like sea without water, with brine only. Minos was Elsewhere, he was already Another. I caressed rhythmically. Minos grew thorns between his legs, like a rose, for protection. My hands bled. I bent lower and bit him, swallowed him whole, sucked him in like a jellyfish. I drank milk between his legs, drank his soul, thirstier than I had ever been before. I could not have quenched that thirst of mine, if I'd swallowed the entire ocean. I had no legs any longer, no arms. I curled up. Mother, standing above me, groaned, contracted. I tried to howl, curled up as I was, but my ears, eyes, nose, and mouth were choked with juices.

Mother screamed. The juices fell away and I opened my eyes and howled.

Minos disappeared forever, running toward the sea, embracing it. A bee flew out of the window.

The swelling on Mother's belly went down.

44. The Reception

Nights I often used to go down to the cellar, where the mummies of the Family lived. They slept on their feet in wooden beds and their eyes never closed.

"We've got insomnia," they all complained. They all talked together as though they had the same mouth.

Their laughter had turned the ceiling rusty, and when they brushed their teeth, owls shot out of their mouths.

"When it's your turn, we'll give you the bed with the view," they said together, and their bones creaked with impatience, for they loved me very much.

I was the only one that knew the mummies lived down there.

"One night, my child, we all broke out of the cemetery and moved in here, taking our beds with us."

"And why did you do that mummies, darling?"

"Because out there, my child, in the earth, we missed Family life," they sang, while dusty tears rolled from their open eyes.

I used to put them to bed—first we all said Our Father Which Art in Heaven, then I kissed them on the cheek, and, turning the light off, said good night.

Today, Grandfather was not feeling very well. When I went to his room in the evening, he had disappeared. Tonight I went down to the cellar and found him with the others. He had just opened his suitcase when I walked in, and was hanging up his clothes from the beams.

"Kassandra, my dear," he said, "please don't tell Grandmother."

We got a big party going and I danced Jesus Goes to England for them. Then we ate and drank to his health. It was a very nice reception.

45. Aunt Samantha Stages a Coup d'État

"Aunt Samantha's staged a coup," Grandmother shrieked. "Only the General can stage one," she explained to me, lowering her voice.

When Aunt Samantha dropped in that afternoon, I got a real fright at the sight of her, so I slipped away and phoned the General.

"General, General, come over quickly. Aunt Samantha's staged a coup d'état. Oh, General, those nice stockings she was wearing, those bracelets and necklaces, they were just to fool us."

"Run along and see if she's wearing dark glasses," the General replied, his voice shaking.

I peeped through the keyhole. She *was* wearing dark glasses.

"She is, General, dark as night."

"I'll be right over. The password will be Sly Sardine. Don't open the door unless you hear it," and he hung up.

I locked Aunt Samantha in the parlor, ran up to my room, put on my helmet and frogman's fins, and hid behind the curtain.

46. Humpty Dumpty

Mina is Minos' Mother. She lives on an island, near our island, on a mountain, with a garden with trees and hanging terraces, all withered.

50 cats live in the house.

She's opened holes in the kitchen, 50 of them, for the cats to go in and out. 50 boxes stand in the parlor for them to sleep in side by side, and she mixes fish and ground meat with her hands for them (I've seen her do it).

At 5 she blows on a red whistle and they charge in like lions. 50 saucers side by side. Wild smells fill the house and spill into the garden.

Mina is almost dead. She's put her teeth away in a velvet box and shows them to me, before we sit down to tea.

"How pretty they are, Mina, sleeping on the red velvet."

She wants me to say the same words always—they're magic words (I know that), and she refuses to close the box again if I forget or make a slip.

She eats bread soaked in milk, even though the house is full of meat for the cats. There's blood dripping everywhere in the kitchen. Mina scrubs it clean so her 50 children won't get soiled.

We're on vacation: Mina, Miss Benbridge, and I. My bedroom is in the attic. Spiders and rats sleep under my bed. In the beginning I was scared; in the beginning, before going to bed, I took a look 37 times to see what they were up to. It took 37 looks to turn the spiders and rats to stone. Later, I got tired of looking, and now I don't see them anymore—it's as though they don't exist. I've made them all invisible, the rats and spiders and all the beasts under my bed.

Miss Benbridge knits in the garden. Mina translates Lao-tse in the kitchen.

We spend our evenings in the parlor. Mina's kept all her books since she was a child, and she's told me their titles too: *Alice's Adventures in Wonderland*, *Winnie-the-Pooh*, and the lightweight ones, as she calls them, Marx, Hegel, Poe, and De Quincey.

Outside, the trees rustle as though they're translating too, turning summer into winter. I'm busy translating the house. I'm calling it *The Menagerie*.

Evenings, the cats climb all over the piano and Mina's knees, while she reads Lao-tse.

One morning they have a fearful scrap; a cat's ear is found in my lap.

"It's so peaceful here," sighs Miss Benbridge, taking her tea and going off to knit under the lemon trees.

After tea, Mina reads *The Turn of the Screw* to me; it's by Mr. Henry James.

"Mina, what does 'screw' mean?"

"A screw, darling," she answers.

"Mina, how do you 'turn' a 'screw'? Mr. James wrote *The Turn of the Screw* on the outside of his book. Mina, how do you 'turn' a 'screw' in a book?"

"Basically, it's a children's book," Mina explains. "You see, their Governess died—look, just like Miss Benbridge, except that *their* Governess was beautiful, with long black hair. Then, out of Love, she turned into a ghost and returned."

By the next page I'm sweating at my belly and at the back of my neck. Still, I love the two little children who live in the book. But Flora's my favorite.

> ... *Miss Jessel stood before us on the opposite bank.*
> *"She's there, you little unhappy thing—there, there,*
> *there, and you see her as well as you see me!"*

"Mina, I'm tired. Why don't you read me Humpty Dumpty?"

"Humpty Dumpty sat on a wall.

"Humpty Dumpty had a great FALL..."

The way Mina reads it, Humpty Dumpty's fall becomes terrifying. I prefer Flora and Miles.

At night, Flora and Miles come to my room. Bending over, the Governess covers me with her wet hair. I've made friends with them.

Flora: black curls, patent-leather bootees. She flutters around my bed, her mouth laughing like a wound.

Miles: blond curls, eyes as black as a bird's insides, hands like an old man's, hands like doves. He sits in the armchair, motionless and serious.

"When I'm bad, I AM bad!"

At the window, behind the pane, the Governess.

I blow out my candle.

"It was I who blew it, dear!"

I fall asleep.

Tomorrow we're going on an excursion across the water to the mainland, to the Lemonwoods.

Mina says: "I'm not feeling very well. It's this pain in my side."

Miss Benbridge says: "It's only for 3 days, my dear."

"And my cats?"

I'm in the garden, looking up at the house.

The Lemonwoods are full of lemon trees. I become a goat, eat lemons and medlars, I roll on the leaves. Here the earth smells earthy, and the sun isn't dark like the one Mina's hung over her house. At night, I sleep with my windows open, Flora and Miles are far away.

I eat chocolates and fruit, I eat earth and sea, I lick the sun too, become a bull, a horse, a sea urchin.

Tomorrow we'll be going back to the island. The night is cooler and I put my jacket on.

We're back in the afternoon, just in time for tea.

The door of the house is wide open. In the kitchen 3 kittens are holding Mina's titties between their front paws, suckling at them. In the corridor, 3 pussy cats are sucking up her eyes. In the parlor, 44 cats are scrapping in her belly. Behind the piano, a leg in a stocking and a shoe.

"They've left it for later, the poor dears," I say to myself, bursting into laughter.

Flora and Miles are on the sofa, watching gravely. I wave to them.

"Humpty Dumpty sat on a wall…" I sing, dancing to the beat.

At the window, behind the pane, the Governess.

47. Exams

My Mother, Kassandra, took me to do some exams, because she wanted me to go to school. They gave us some white and hairy bits of paper and told us to draw a tree.

With a small doubt going around in my head, I chewed at the end of my pencil: I couldn't remember what colors I'd seen on the trees and all around. I picked up the red and made a cherry-red tree on a blue hill. All around, the sky was black and thick. All the children passed the exams except me.

When we left the school, I looked carefully at the colors running up and down the trees. By the time I got home, I'd forgotten them.

48. God and the Devil

"Kassandra, dear, tell me what you heard in Church."

Uncle Harílaos is thinking of leaving the earth, so he's preparing his journey carefully.

"When are you leaving, Uncle Harílaos?"

"I'm waiting for the weather to improve, but I haven't decided where I want to go yet."

Uncle Harílaos sucks his finger and holds it up to see which way the wind is blowing.

"Uncle Harílaos, ever since I had Holy Communion, I've loved God as much as I love my friend Hercules."

"Aha, Kassandra dear, I do love it so when the priest dips his silver spoon in his Holy Pot and we're all waiting in line for him to stuff it in our mouths."

"Well, Uncle Harílaos, I'll tell you something: when I grow up, I'm going to become a priest. I'll travel all over the world with my spoon and people will run after me, crying and begging me for a gulp, and the earth will be so full of Christians that they won't be able to fit in Paradise, so God will have to build a new Paradise, a more modern one, with a telephone and a swimming pool and rooms with a view down to earth."

"Oh, Kassandra dear, that's where I want to go."

I love Uncle Harílaos so much that I want to give him a fright.

"And the Devil will be jealous, you know, and he'll build himself a new Hell, with lovely fires and Persian rugs, and the Christians will do all sorts of mischief on earth so they can go to Hell, and the Bad will become Good, and Paradise will be jammed with murderers, and nobody will dare go out at night in the garden. But in Hell the Christians will sit all around the fires, roasting chestnuts."

"In that case, where will I be going?"

Uncle Harílaos is in a real fright. I take his head in my hands.

"The Devil has given birth to a baby too. He's thrown it down to earth to save us. It has green eyes, it makes up and dresses like a woman, it has red hair—I know it well, Uncle. Look what it did to me last night, when it kissed me." I ring Grandmother's silver bell. "Do you want to meet him, Uncle Harílaos?"

Peter opens the door.

"Peter, my good man, bring us something to drink, if you please."

49. The Word

One morning, I woke up dumb, still as a clock, waves turning back on themselves.

One morning, I couldn't hear. I quarreled with sounds. I turned into a table. I turned transparent.

It rained from the sky, and the raindrops turned to tears on my cheeks. I chewed words, so heavy I couldn't lift them, turned to pebbles in my belly. I changed shapes constantly. (Dumb) words came out of my mouth, and the air around me tore them in pieces.

Letters turned to reptiles. The only thing I could hear was my heart: Bang—bang, bang—bang. I knew no other tune. I looked around me and listened to my heart: Bang—bang, bang—bang. I forgot everything else.

People spoke to me.

"Bang bang, bang—bang," I replied.

At night, forgotten words tried to reach me. I listened with my skin. Words tore my skin off, crept inside me, and nestled down. I was a mass of wounds. When I opened my mouth in front of the mirror, beasts lay asleep in my throat; they'd made it their home.

I was in a faraway land. Bang—bang, bang—bang. I'd forgotten everything else.

T—K—P—X. They were driving me crazy.

A—R. Balsam.

Grandmother spoke: Not a squeak.

Mother spoke: I bled.

Peter: He knew. He lulled the beasts to sleep.

"My little cabbage, I'll take you away from here."

T—K—P—X: "Peter, don't leave me."

"We'll go to the island."

Grandmother was cleaning Grandfather's pipe: "Would you like a cup of tea?"

On the island we closed the doors, shutters, and curtains, and stuffed black paper in the chinks. Then we undressed and went to bed for years, months, and weeks.

"Bang—bang, bang—bang."

"Bang—bang," he answered.

I suckled Peter. He turned into a woman. I suckled him to fall asleep. Yesterday a spider sprang from my mouth. I was shrinking. I suckled him every 3 hours, lizards died in my belly.

Peter became a cave, and I lost my teeth.

Peter's breasts grew. He opened out, and I shrank.

We drove sounds away. The ones that were left we tamed and turned into dogs.

In the dark, in his arms, Peter took me for a stroll around the house.

"Bang—bang, bang—bang," something inside me began to respond.

A vein ran from Peter's heart to mine, and I was filled with tunes.

Naked, we stood in front of the mirror.

"Open your mouth," he said. "You!" he said.

He licked me in the mirror.

"I!" he said, pointing to himself.

He turned into a shelter and water.

One morning a word tottered on the brink.

"Come on, my little cabbage, it'll hurt. It'll hurt me too."

I crawled into his belly and grabbed hold. It was so peaceful there that I curled up and fell asleep, but Peter was pushing out, rhythmically.

"Bang—bang, bang—bang. Peter, let me stay in here."

His body arched forward and I shot out.

The windows were open: air, and the sun warming my hair. I opened my eyes. Something fluttered in my mouth.

A word.

50. One Afternoon in July, Friday

One afternoon in July, Friday, I slipped out of the house.

Grandmother was sleeping, her dizzy spells keeping her company. On Tuesday, she'd bought a black mask for her eyes so that she wouldn't see anything. Faní went off to the grocer's to buy some flypaper because the kitchen was swarming with flies, even though Peter had fitted screens over the windows. The flies just slid through and stuck to the cheese and the refrigerator.

One afternoon in July, Friday, I hid behind a tree in front of the big church. A Lady in red was sitting on the pavement, vomiting.

4 coffin men brought out a coffin and put it on the ground in front of her. She leaned over and vomited into the coffin. Then they put the lid on and all the Relatives came out of the church, holding long tapers and wreaths. They stood all around the coffin, staring at it. They were all in red and the Ladies had big red kerchiefs on their heads.

I crept closer and hid behind another tree right beside the Lady. I saw then that it was black they were wearing and that it was the trees all around that were cherry red.

The coffin men lifted the coffin into a long red car, resting it on something soft—feathers, I think. The Lady got in the car and sat near the coffin, by the window.

I tapped at the window.

"Who have you killed, Madame?" I asked.

She lowered the window, turned her head, and vomited over my frock.

51. Grandmother Leaves by Train on an Afternoon in July, Saturday

She began preparing her suitcases a month before, taking all her dresses and silk stockings with her—Faní ironed them all, one by one.

"65 pairs," she told me in the kitchen.

She took her overcoats, furs, shoes, and all her summer clothes as well. For her dog Buddha she took his coats, bootees, bathing costume, sporting outfit for his morning constitutional, and his Habit Rouge Guerlain perfume.

She took her gold, pearls, and rings. And she took rose water to refresh herself with on the train. She also took the black mask for her eyes so she wouldn't see anything.

Faní and Peter and I took her to the station.

"Look, Kassandra, dear, I'm wearing my big diamond. I'm afraid it might get stolen if I leave it in the jewel case. Peter, do you think someone might sneak into my compartment at night and saw my finger off? You see, I'll be wearing my black mask and I'll have my ears stuffed with wax so as not to hear the wheels. So do you think someone might sneak in without my getting wind of him?"

Peter laughed, then Grandmother laughed, then I laughed too.

Grandmother climbed on board the train, which began to pull out of the station. She put her arm out of the window to say goodbye, and I could see the diamond sparkling way out as far as the bend.

The trees all around were cherry red.

52. The Ghost

"Oh, Faní, darling, I love you so!" I think as I creep down the stairs on tiptoe so that Peter won't hear me. He'd be very angry if he found out I'm going down to Faní to get into bed with her and cuddle up to her.

He wants me to run only to him, and I've given him my word that he'll always be my Mother. On the other hand, Faní would get angry too if she knew about St. Sebastian. She must never know how brightly Peter sparkles when he stands in the rain, how beautiful he is when he puts on his frock and orange curls.

I sit on the stairs, take out my marbles and count them. 1 for Peter, 1 for Faní. I share them out carefully so I won't forget.

How hard it is to love. It's like cutting a kiss in two, like separating the lentils from the horse beans. Sometimes I forget: I kiss Faní, thinking it's Peter, but Peter's spying from behind the curtain. I'm lucky he's asleep now so he'll never learn I've been to Faní tonight. The house is dark, so even if someone sees me, I'll say I'm a Ghost.

I go down another step and accidentally spill my marbles. They scatter all over the place, some of them rolling into the slit of light under Faní's door. I bounce down the remaining steps, open the door, and run in to get them back.

Someone's covering Faní on the bed.

"Státhis!" I shout, getting closer.

I see Peter's hair shining on the pillow. Faní's arms are

holding him tight around the waist, and her legs are around him like an octopus. They're both breathing and moving like flowers in the sea; it's so nice that I want to play as well. They shout and the room shakes.

I squat down on the floor next to the bed and stare. Peter's leg touches my hair. He leaps up and grabs me.

"What are you doing here? What are you doing?" he shouts, bundling me out of the door.

Sitting on my step again, I burst into tears.

"Why are you so upset, my little cabbage? We were just learning words."

"I've lost them," I cry, and with my finger point into the darkness where my marbles have rolled.

53. An Errand from Paris

September, Sunday.

The house is empty.

Státhis and Faní have gone to the sea for a fish dinner, Peter's off to the Casino, and Miss Benbridge left for England yesterday.

I like being alone in the house.

I switch on the 7 radios, from the kitchen to Grandmother's bedroom. I switch off all the telephones, except Faní's down in the kitchen.

I put on the 7 record players and dance The Death of the Swan, The Sylphide, and 1 or 2 of my own. The house becomes mine, except that Grandmother's clothes are gone and I can't wear the high heels and fur coat.

I'm in the middle of dancing one of my own, when I hear the phone ringing down in the kitchen. 4 floors: I'll never have time to switch off the radios and record players. I dash down to answer it, pick up the receiver, but hear nothing. I switch off Faní's radio, next to the telephone.

"Allô, allô! Ici Hôpital Saint-Sulpice."

"Hello! How are you? Could you please hold the line while I run up and switch the radio off in the parlor?"

I run up and run down again.

"Allô? On vous telephone de Paris."

I'm glad I know a bit of French; it must be Grandmother from Paris.

"Allô, allô? Grandmother? Could you hold the line

119

while I run upstairs and switch the record player off in Mother's room? I can't hear you."

I come running back.

"*Allô?* Grandmother, is that you? Could you hold the line while I switch the radio off in the dining room?"

I come sliding back down on the banisters.

"*Allô? Ici Hôpital Saint-Sulpice. Je vous passe l'Ambassadeur de Grece.*"

I swell out like a peacock.

"Hello there, Mr. Ambassador! Grandmother's away, but do tell me what you want and I'll make it into a letter for her."

The house goes dumb.

"*Allô! Je vous passe l'Ambassadeur de Grece.*"

"But you've already said that 7 times, Madame. Please give me the Ambassador. I am a member of the Royal Court."

"Good morning, Madame. What coffin would you like us to order?"

"Black and gold, with iron handles made of emeralds, and velvet silk inside, if you please."

"Yes," the Ambassador replies. "We have embalmed her too."

"Embalm away, embalm away," I sing out. "Turn her into a flower, turn her into a doll. But just tell me the name of this Lady so I can make it into a letter to my Grandmother."

The Ambassador goes dumb.

I put the receiver down on Faní's table and bend down to pick Grandmother's name off the floor. I want to put it back in the receiver.

"*Allô, allô? Ici Hopital Saint-Sulpice. Allô?*"

I switch on the radios and record players, close the shutters and windows, and draw the velvet curtains.

I dance St. Sebastian in the Swans' Lake, the sky black and thick, the trees all around cherry red, and I draw the hill blue.

54. The Shadow

Like every Thursday, I went to Uncle Harílaos' to play with the long red train Aunt Pátra had given him for his birthday.

We stretched out on the floor, put trees and schools and houses around the rails.

But this time Uncle Harílaos wasn't in the mood to play. He kept clutching at his throat and loosening his tie.

"Do you know how to tie knots?" he asked.

"Miss Benbridge has taught me some lovely ones," I said.

He went to the kitchen and brought back a thick rope. We practiced a lot of knots on it, then we went to the bedroom, hung the rope from the ceiling, and Uncle Harílaos put the other end around his neck. I wanted to play the game too.

"Some other time. It's my turn today," he said. "If you help me play a nice game today, it'll be your turn next Thursday, I promise."

We tried lots of times, but sometimes the rope was too short and other times too long, till finally Uncle Harílaos burst into tears and sat on the floor sobbing.

I sat down next to him, and he, taking me in his arms, asked me to tell him a story.

"I'll tell you the one about the Birdman," I said. "The Birdman lived on a high mountain and loved the Fishwoman very much. But they could never manage to meet each other, you see, because he couldn't get in the water and she couldn't fly. That's why the Bird always flew over the sea, and the Fish always followed in the waves, until, finally, the Bird covered it and became its Shadow. Before that none of us had a Shadow. We walked about quite plain and we were cold too. But from that time on, the Shadow was born, and now we all have one to keep us company."

Uncle Harílaos' sobs became even louder.

"I don't even have a Shadow. I don't have anything. I'm the only one that doesn't have one. There, look, I don't have one!" he wept, pointing to the white wall, which was white.

It was dark by now, so we switched on the light.

"Kassandra, let's try again."

He climbed on the stool, put the rope around his neck, and once again I pulled the stool from under his feet.

This time, Uncle Harílaos started flying around the room, moving his arms there and here so he could get a flying start.

Then I saw his Shadow flying on the wall, keeping him company.

"Uncle Harílaos, look, look there!"

But his eyes had gone white, and I thought how I'd never seen such a lovely Shadow in my whole life, dancing there on the wall, while Uncle Harílaos, his arms stretched out, tried and tried to catch it.

55. The Baby

The doctor opened my legs and stuck his head in. He was looking for the baby, which was giving him the slip, because it didn't want to come out, especially in this manner.

"Don't worry, we'll corner it sooner or later," he said, winking his left eye.

Wailing loudly, the baby kept grabbing at the walls of my belly. Its tears trickled between my legs, stinging me. This made me angry.

"Get out!" I told it. "Get out! If you don't get out on your own, I'll give a huge squeeze with my muscles and catapult you out."

At this point the doctor got angry too and shoved in a lancet to finish it off. The baby took off at a run, grabbed hold of my liver, and took cover a bit farther up.

"So we're playing hide-and-seek now, are we?" shrieked the nurse, who was bathed in blood.

The baby was now tickling my throat, which made me burst into laughter. Pulling a flashlight from his pocket, the doctor shoved it in my mouth.

"I've found it, I've found it!" he called out.

The nurse lent a hand and they managed to grab it by the leg. They put 2 hooks in my mouth to keep it open, and the doctor, with his freshly polished lancet, got down to work. First he sliced off its leg and tossed it into a saucepan, then the head. The baby was laughing, but I couldn't laugh because my mouth was full of blood and red snot and was being stretched, moreover, like a catapult.

All of the baby had been brought out by now, and it lay shredded in a white saucepan.

After the doctor had put some gauze in my mouth to stop the red snot from running, Mother took me by the one hand and Father by the other, and we returned home.

56. First Day at School

It's still pitch dark but I'm already up. Starched uniform, shiny white collar, an empty schoolbag deep as a trunk. At the very bottom of it, there's a pencil with a quite fabulous point, and a sheet of paper with lines. The house is snoring.

So, in my bright new disguise, I climb downstairs on the tips of my toes so as not to wake the Family. I creep past Grandmother's room, Grandfather's, Mother's, the kitchen.

"Faní, they're all asleep. Faní, I'm scared."

"I'll take you there myself, darling. I won't leave you alone for a second."

She warms my milk.

"Do you want some of yesterday's halvah?"

"Faní, I'm scared."

It's The First Day, and they've all forgotten about it.

Faní and I are outside the school 2 hours early. The night's as black as a rook. We buy doughnuts.

"Faní, when I get back at noon, I'll bring you a bucketful of letters and a few numbers."

Dawn.

Mothers begin to arrive with their children. The children are clutching their Mothers with one hand, their schoolbags with the other, and there are tears in their eyes.

"Faní, should I be crying too? Oh, I can't be bothered. Anyway, I don't have anything for the snot."

Bells ring and gates fly open. A huge concrete playground and, along one wall, windows with yellow lights. One tree in the middle of the playground.

"My school's like a bad egg, Faní."

"You'll get used to it," she says, lighting a cigarette.

They're all crying now, Mothers and children together, in time. They stop for a moment, then start again like steam engines. In the pauses, I hear the traffic and the doughnut vendor.

"Doughnuts, doughnuts! Fresh doughnuts!"

Across the road, someone's playing a piano.

A Gentleman, as serious as an eraser, walks out of the building. He blows a whistle 3 times and we fall into lines.

"First Grade, over by the lavatories!"

When I hear my name, I run to the end of the line. The Mothers fall into line too and leave.

In class: the teacher is sitting behind the table. I can see her thighs right up to her belly button. Just below her panties, 2 purple suspenders, which are so tight that the flesh tumbles over them like a hanging garden.

"Open your schoolbags! Get your pencils out! Behave yourselves!"

We become angels.

"And now, tell me your namey-wameys so I'll know who you are."

Yannis

Fotiní

Phaedra

Boúlis

Patroklos

Antigone

Ka-Ka-Ka-Ka-s-s-s-sandra

"Come and sit in the front row, my child. I am Miss

Ada, your teacher. I shall teach you to read, write, and think. We'll be telling little stories, cutting frogs in two, and in general having a wonderful time together.

"Now, I want each little child to tell me something he or she likes, and I want him to put it in a nice, clean little phrase. How about you, my child?" she asks, looking straight at me.

"Fa-Fa-Fa-ní's s e-e-e-elastic sto-sto-sto-ckings."

The class rolls about helplessly.

Miss Ada looks at her watch.

"Next," she says tenderly.

Later: "And now, children, I'll give out your reading books and read you some words. Words are letters stuck together, and they also make a noise."

Standing up, she holds the book out like a loaf, and begins:

"Ma-ri-a-is-play-ing. Pe-ter-is-naugh-ty."

I'm sure she's playing some trick on us—I hear phrases like these every day, and, what's more, her stammer's even worse than mine.

"And now, little children, I want you to tell me a little phrase. And make sure you separate the syllables. I want to hear those syl-la-bles-ring."

Yannis: "I-love-my-Mum-my."

Phaedra: "I-love-my-Dad-dy."

Me: "The-P-P-P-Pope-is-a-p-p-p-pig."

Miss Ada's curl comes undone and falls, withered, down her face.

"I shall phone your Mother."

I'll make syllables so as not to stammer.

"She-is-in-Pa-ris."

"Your Grandmother."

"She-is-a-sleep."

"Your Father."

"He-does-not-e-xist."

Miss Ada thinks.

"Recess," she says.

We run into the playground. I'm about to bite into my doughnut, when Miss Ada calls from the window: "Everybody inside!" and I sit down again at my desk.

"Now, little children, we're going to learn numbers. Take out your squared paper, erasers, and pencils."

I'm in the very front desk. Miss Ada's curl is in my nostril, and Miss Ada's thighs are in my mouth; Miss Ada's curl, like her thigh, is twisted around.

I gaze at the tree in the playground.

"We have numbers, children, so as to be able to count." Miss Ada puts 4 pears on the table.

"1, 2, 3, 4," she says. "Yannis, you take 1. Kassandra, how many do we have left?"

"1, 2, 3, 4. Yannis has the 4th."

Miss Ada's curl sighs:

"My child, if Yannis, takes 1, we have 3 left over."

"And that makes 4, together with the 1 Yannis has."

"My child, we are doing subtraction."

Tears come to my eyes. I don't understand.

"Miss Ada, why are you so bad to me? Even if Yannis eats the pear, we'll still have 4 pears. Together with the 1 in his belly, we'll still have 4, only the 4th will be down the toilet."

Miss Ada's curl flickers.

"Yannis, dear boy, how many will be left over if we take 1 away?"

"3."

Yannis is fat, and on his desk he's got 10 erasers and 20 pencils.

I'm sure they're all mad in this place. What about the 4th pear? If I let this 4th pear get away from me, Grandmother will die for good.

"Granny dear," I tell her, "I shan't let you drop in the lavatory bowl."

I think of Grandfather too, all alone in the cellar, and I start explaining at the top of my voice:

"2 and 2 make 2 and 2, and not 4. Join 2 Grandfathers to 2 other Grandfathers and they make 2 and 2 Grandfathers, not 4. Or rather, they make 1, 2, 3, 4. If you stir them all together in a saucepan and boil them, then, yes, the 1, 2, 3, 4 Grandfathers will become 1 Grandfather, round and swollen out, and maybe younger too."

Faní's waiting for me at the gate.

"How was school?"

"Very good. I've learned to speak, answer, and think in syllables."

"Then why are you crying?"

"It's the syllables. It hurts when I cut the words in two."

"You'll get used to it," Faní says. "You'll get used to it."

"Karapanou writes of childhood with such lyric ferocity; her Kassandra and the Wolf *has [a] jagged fantastic substance ... with a vicious pre-pubescent sexual element chillingly added."*
— **John Updike**, **New York Times**

Margarita Karapanou's Kassandra and the Wolf was first published in 1974, and went on to become a contemporary classic in Greece, receive international acclaim, and establish its 28-year-old author as an intensely original new talent, who garnered comparisons to Proust and Schulz.

Six-year-old Kassandra is given a doll: "I put her to sleep in her box, but first I cut off her legs and arms so she'd fit," she tells us, "Later, I cut her head off too, so she wouldn't be so heavy. Now I love her very much." Kassandra is an unforgettable narrator, a perfect, brutal guide to childhood as we've never seen it—a journey that passes through the looking glass but finds the darkest corners of the real world. This edition brings *Kassandra and the Wolf* back into print at last—a tour de force and, as Karapanou liked to call it, a scary monster of a book.

ISBN: 978-1-62371-697-4   US $16.95

51695

9 781623 716974

INTERLINK BOOKS
An imprint of
Interlink Publishing Group, Inc.
www.interlinkbooks.com